Praise for Cat Johnson's
Bucked

"Hot diggity dog, do I love me some cowboys, and no one writes about em' better than Cat Johnson... Fans of Ms. Johnson's previous stories will enjoy Bucked, especially if they have a yen for Mustang like I do. The material flows nicely, the continuation is something new and unexpected, and the journey is one worth taking."

~ *Whipped Cream Long and Short Reviews*

"Cat Johnson continues to be one of my favorite authors. Whether it is in military, contemporary or the cowboy arena she definitely knows her alpha males... Bucked is a highly erotic story that has a ménage, a d/S and some regular cowboy loving in it but you will love the plot line that goes with it."

~ *Joyfully Reviewed*

"Mustang is the kind of man who would make a woman dream of happily ever after... This story is both heart warming and at times a little heart wrenching, but you won't want to miss it. It will make you want to come back for the next book in the Studs in Spurs series. I can't wait..."

~ *Veiled Secrets Reviews*

"BUCKED introduces all new characters you'll fall in love with...and gives readers the opportunity to revisit all of the characters you know and love from UNRIDDEN. Cat Johnson once again proves she's an author who has staying power. I can hardly wait to find out what her next story will involve."

~ *Romance Junkies*

Look for these titles by
Cat Johnson

Now Available:

Rough Stock

Studs in Spurs Series
Unridden
Bucked
Ride

Red, Hot and Blue Series
Trey
Jack
Jimmy

Bucked

Cat Johnson

SAMHAIN PUBLISHING

Samhain Publishing, Ltd.
577 Mulberry Street, Suite 1520
Macon, GA 31201
www.samhainpublishing.com

Bucked
Copyright © 2010 by Cat Johnson
Print ISBN: 978-1-60504-923-6
Digital ISBN: 978-1-60504-900-7

Editing by Heidi Moore
Cover by Amanda Kelsey

First Samhain Publishing, Ltd. electronic publication: February 2010
First Samhain Publishing, Ltd. print publication: December 2010

Dedication

Nikki—who loves Mustang and Chase as much as I do.

Mike—for his help, inspiration, patient computer tech support, sympathetic ear and steady belief in me and for allowing me to borrow the details of his real-life bull-riding injury for my story.

Gary—for being my beta reader no matter what the genre and my unfailing supporter in both work and life.

As with all my works of fiction, any liberties taken with the facts or mistakes made are purely my own.

Prologue

Sage Beckett dropped to her knees and peered past the dust bunnies beneath the bed. Pushing aside the white eyelet dust ruffle, she squinted into the darkness searching for what she knew was there somewhere.

"Hey there, Little Bit. Whatcha doing under there?"

The sound of a familiar voice had her heart pounding and not only because he'd startled her. Sage's pulse routinely raced from simply thinking about the boy who lived on the next street over.

She swiveled her head to find those piercing blue eyes that melted her from the inside out focused on her.

"Um. Nothing." Guiltily, she let the bedcovers fall back into place and jumped to her feet.

"Where's Rosemary? Do you know?" Michael leaned casually against the doorframe as if he had no clue what his mere presence did to her pubescent body.

Of course, he had no idea how he affected her, how she felt about him. To him she was just Rosemary's little sister, the middle schooler who followed them around the house and who they were forced to let tag along to their high school games. Michael would never see her as a woman, would never know the very real and adult feelings she had for him. Not as long as Rosemary was around anyway.

"I don't know. She's not home from school yet." Which was why Sage had been under her sister's bed looking for Rosemary's diary. Her sister would never tell her what was happening with Michael, but that diary did.

"Do you think your grandmother has any of those empanadas she made yesterday left in the fridge?" Michael's devilish grin drew Sage's gaze to his perfectly shaped lips and made her immediately think what it would feel like to kiss them.

Rosemary had kissed those lips. In fact, her sister and the object of Sage's secret affection had not only kissed. They'd done more than that already and Sage had read every heartbreaking detail.

She pressed a hand to her churning stomach. The pain of what she'd read the last time she'd snooped in Rosemary's diary was still very present. The fear of what she'd read next made her ill.

Her eyes dropped to his hand braced on the door molding. What she'd give to feel that hand touching her own breasts.

Ha! What breasts? Rosemary was the sister who had the boobs in the family. Sage had nothing. Nothing that could attract Michael compared to what Rosemary had.

"Little Bit, you feeling okay?"

His words kicked her into action. What was the good in wallowing in self-pity? He was here. Rosemary wasn't. For now at least he was all hers. "Yeah. I'm fine. Come on to the kitchen. I'll heat up those empanadas for you."

His face broke into a wide smile. "You're the best."

As she led the way to the other room, Sage prayed one day soon Michael would realize *that* was the absolute truth and forget all about Rosemary.

Reaching into the fridge, Sage pushed aside the lettuce and grabbed the foil packet she'd stashed there the night before.

She always remembered to hide some empanadas for Michael, knowing he'd be there looking for leftovers the next day. On the other hand, Rosemary obviously couldn't remember to even come home right after class. It was pretty apparent to Sage which one of them deserved him more and it wasn't her older sister.

Michael scraped the kitchen chair across the floor and straddled it so he faced her while she reheated the food.

Knowing he was watching, Sage wished even more keenly her body would mature and catch up with the rest of her. She was doing advanced schoolwork that put her on the level with kids two years older than her. Emotionally she was an adult, capable of caring for him far better than her selfish sister. So why didn't her teeth get straight already so the braces could come off? And when would she be old enough to get contact lenses and ditch her ugly glasses? Some boobs would be nice too. Not huge, but enough to catch Michael's attention.

"Did I tell you? I got that summer job."

Sage spun away from the counter to face him. "You did? The one on the ranch?"

"Yup. That's the one."

"That's so great. I know you really wanted it."

He laughed. "Oh yeah. I was desperate. My father was looking into getting me a job working with him every day for the summer."

"That would have been bad." Sage cringed at the thought. She couldn't count the number of times Michael had shown up at their back door red-faced and sullen after a fight with his father.

"Yeah, tell me about it. Anyway, some of the job will be stuff like cleaning out the barn, but I'll also get to learn how to handle the stock. And the guys I'll be working with said they'll teach me how to ride bulls like they do."

"Really? They ride bulls?"

He leaned forward, the excitement evident in the expression on his sun-browned face. "Hell, yeah. Do you know how much money they make? One guy rode in a competition last weekend and won. He got five thousand bucks and this really cool belt buckle."

"Five thousand. Wow. That's really good."

"I know." His head bobbed with an enthusiastic nod. "I could work all summer with my father and not make even near that."

Michael's entire body visibly vibrated with his excitement. So much so she hated to bring up the next question. "Have you told your parents about getting the job yet?"

Eyes lowered, he began picking at a chip in the edge of the kitchen table. "No. I guess I have to soon though. I'm supposed to start work this weekend."

Sage's mood fell right along with his. Her guilt at having smothered his good mood with the mention of his parents overwhelmed her.

The toaster oven dinged and the aroma of her grandmother's home cooking filled the kitchen, telling her the leftovers were done heating. Grateful for the distraction, Sage grabbed a potholder and pulled the hot tray of meat-filled pastries out. She slid them onto a plate and turned toward Michael, hoping the sight of his favorite food would cheer him up again after she'd depressed him.

Putting the dish on the table, she resisted the urge to brush her hand over his.

"Hey. Do you want to come over for dinner after your first day of work? Maybe Grams can make something special and we can celebrate."

His eyes lifted. "Okay."

"Celebrate what?" Rosemary blew in through the screen door and dropped her bag on the table, narrowly missing the plate of food.

"Michael got a job working with bulls at a ranch." Sage shared that news with the enthusiasm it deserved, knowing how much Michael had wanted that job.

She only hoped his father would let him keep it when he heard what he'd be doing. His son cleaning stalls and handling farm stock would not make Mr. Jackson happy. Riding bulls would be even worse. Sage knew the man enough to know that for a fact.

"A ranch? Doing what? Shoveling manure? Lovely." Rosemary let out a snort. "Bobby's working at his father's company for the summer."

Popping in a big mouthful of food, Michael chewed and swallowed. "Wearing a business suit, talking on the phone while trapped inside in an office all day selling insurance? Yeah, that sounds like a really fun way to spend the summer."

"Whatever." Her sister rolled her eyes before they narrowed in on the last empanada as it disappeared into Michael's mouth. Rosemary spun to face Sage. "I thought there were no leftovers last night. I wanted seconds and when I asked you, you said they were all gone."

Maybe if her lazy sister had gotten up from the table and actually walked to the stove to look for herself she would have found them. As it was, Sage was glad she hadn't so she could save these for Michael. "Um, I found a few on another tray Grams left warming in the oven. Sorry."

Behind Rosemary, Michael smiled and rose. "Sorry, Rose. All gone. You ready to go study for that test?"

"Yeah. Grab my book bag, will you?" Rosemary breezed out of the kitchen empty-handed and headed down the hall toward her room without a backward glance.

"Sure thing." Grabbing the bag, Michael winked at Sage. "Thanks, Little Bit. Those hit the spot."

She felt her cheeks grow warm. "You're welcome."

Then he was gone too. She heard Rosemary's bedroom door close behind him. No doubt they'd lock it and there would be more than studying going on. Sage swallowed to rid herself of the acid taste in her throat.

Life simply wasn't fair.

Chapter One

Mustang Jackson tightened the buckle on the last of the six leather chap straps wrapped around his thighs. Straightening, he glanced at the chutes. One of the younger kids was getting situated on the back of a particularly rank bull. The animal kept hopping, banging against the metal rails. Judging by the expression on the rider's face the animal's behavior was starting to unnerve him.

Normally Mustang would jump right up there and try to help. As a seasoned rider with many years in the pro circuit under his belt he tried to mentor the younger guys whenever he could, but right now he had his own ride to get ready for.

Eventually, a stock contractor climbed up to deal with the animal and Mustang could stop worrying about the other rider and concentrate on himself.

He pulled a leather glove onto his riding hand and wrapped a strip of tape tightly around the top of the glove at his wrist. Tearing off the length of adhesive with his teeth, Mustang glanced at the action in the chute again. The rider was up off the bull, straddling the rails as the stock guy adjusted the flank strap around the animal's hindquarters.

Slade wandered over as Mustang stretched out his triceps one at a time while watching the proceedings.

"You up next?"

"One more after him, then me." Anxious to get on his bull and get this ride over with, Mustang let out a long, frustration-filled breath of air. "It looks like this one could take awhile."

"Yup, it sure does." Slade nodded. "You ready to take on Ballbreaker?"

"I'm always ready." Mustang hooked the heel of one booted foot on the bottom rail while he waited for God knew how long. He winced as he felt the painful tug of muscles in an area he'd rather not have pain.

"That groin pull from last week still giving you trouble, or did you reinjure yourself during last night's activities?"

Mustang never could hide shit from Slade, which was one reason he never played poker against him.

"For your information, smart ass, there were no 'activities' last night." Unfortunately, because he could sure go for some activity in that department. "The groin's just a little tender still. I'll be fine."

Slade shot him a sidelong glance. "I hope so."

So did Mustang. They both knew he had better be on the top of his game to ride last season's Bull of the Year.

Ballbreaker may have dumped Mustang in the dirt after two seconds the one and only time he'd been on him, but the animal had given Slade a lot worse during their matchup.

Mustang glanced again at the chutes and saw the rider still wasn't ready. He let his gaze roam the crowd while he waited. "Did Jenna get a good seat?"

"Yeah. She's not in the front row but at least she's in the VIP section. When I left her she was trying to ask one of the Brazilian rider's wives questions for research for her next book."

He laughed. "That sounds like typical Jenna. Curious as ever."

"Yup, only Jenna was trying to talk to her in what sounded like Spanish she learned in high school. I didn't have the heart to tell her Brazilians speak Portuguese."

Mustang laughed. "Ah, man. She's gonna be pissed at you for not telling her."

Slade grinned. "That's okay. She can get as pissed off as she wants. I'll enjoy the make-up sex."

"Yeah, yeah. Rub it in." He shook his head. There'd been a time they'd both enjoyed sex with Jenna. That cozy threesome had happened before Mustang had seen how she and Slade were falling for each other. He'd bowed out so they could be together but that didn't mean he still didn't look back fondly upon those times. He was a red-blooded, healthy male in his sexual prime after all.

"There's Ballbreaker." Tipping his head, Slade nodded toward their right.

Slade's announcement dispelled any thoughts of sex and drew all of Mustang's attention to where the stockmen were loading the massive bull into a chute on the other side.

"They're loading him for a left-side delivery?" Mustang frowned.

Slade watched the procedure too. "Looks like. He was in a right-side chute for both of our rides."

Mustang nodded. "Exactly, and he spun to the right first both of those times."

"So what will he do now that the chute's opening on the other side of him?" Slade raised a brow in question.

"That's what I'd like to know." Mustang searched the immediate area, hoping to find the stock manager. He spotted him talking to the television interviewer just as the kid who'd been taking his time messing around in the chute finally took off for his ride.

There wasn't time to be wandering around asking about Ballbreaker's habits. Mustang had to get his ass on that bull or risk a penalty for delaying the competition. There was already one other rider up on his bull and waiting for the arena to be clear so he could ride, then it would be Mustang's turn.

"Shit. I guess we'll soon find out which way he'll turn 'cause I gotta go." Mustang jumped down, ignoring the pull of muscles in his groin.

Stepping off the rail, Slade grinned. "Wouldn't be any fun if things were easy, you know."

Mustang let out a snort. "Yeah, you and Ballbreaker had tons of fun together in Tulsa. I'm kind of hoping for a little less fun tonight."

Slade strode toward the chute next to him. "Hey, I had a ninety-point ride and walked away with the second-place paycheck. I'd call that fun."

The harder the bull, the higher the score. If you rode him to the buzzer and didn't look like a sack of potatoes while doing it, of course.

"True, and you got that bonus ride to the hospital too." Letting the green-eyed monster take over, Mustang glanced at the VIP section where the riders' families sat, knowing Jenna was seated there somewhere. "I guess if Jenna was willing to tend to me the same way she took care of you after your ride, I wouldn't mind a trip around the arena underneath Ballbreaker's hooves either."

It was so easy to tease Slade, especially about Jenna. The man had a jealous streak a mile wide. With one quick glance at his friend, Mustang noted Slade was no longer smiling, but he sure as hell was as he climbed up onto the rails.

Mustang regretted the smart-ass comment he'd made to

Slade about Jenna the moment he climbed onto the bull's back. Maybe it was bad Karma or something, not that Mustang particularly believed in that kind of shit, but the moment he lowered his ass onto Ballbreaker things felt off.

For one, the damn bull kept sitting back on his haunches, leaning against the end of the chute. Mustang was familiar with this little trick from his other matchup against Ballbreaker, but it didn't make it any less annoying or easier to deal with now. It was hard to get settled on a bony back that sloped to the rear.

Then there was the left-hand versus right-hand delivery issue. When the gate opened to Ballbreaker's left, would the bull start to spin left? Or did he always go right, no matter what?

Mustang drew in a deep breath. How the hell could he know what this bull was thinking? If Ballbreaker was thinking anything at all besides how to get the rider off his back.

He wound the bull rope tightly around his left hand twice and then wove it between his fingers, trying not to think about how that method was often referred to as the "suicide wrap" because it sometimes didn't release when the rider fell off. At the moment, Mustang was more concerned about staying on than falling off.

About as settled as he was going to get, he figured delaying wasn't helping any. Even though Ballbreaker was still all bunched up in the back of the chute, Mustang nodded for the gate to open and they were off.

He needn't have worried about the left versus right-hand delivery, because Ballbreaker didn't spin to the left or to the right. Instead, the bull ran out into the arena and made one giant leap high into the air. Landing hard, Ballbreaker let his head drop low while his legs kicked straight out behind. Mustang felt the bull's incredible power as he twisted beneath him, every snap and turn intended to dislodge the rider.

Mustang concentrated on keeping his free arm raised and his weight centered as Ballbreaker changed it up and started spinning left in the direction of Mustang's riding hand.

With the amazing way things sometimes seemed to move in slow motion, Mustang heard the eight-second buzzer, reached down and effortlessly unwrapped the rope from around his left hand. Freed, he jumped to the ground.

He ran for the rails after landing on his feet in a perfect dismount. He hopped up, grabbed the top and waited in relative safety as the bullfighters worked to chase Ballbreaker out of the arena toward the stock pens in back.

Still in awe at how easy the ride had been, Mustang jumped down once the arena was clear, landing with a puff of dust beneath his feet. With his ungloved hand, he pulled his mouthguard out and stashed it in a pocket, grinning the entire time over his great ride.

One of the bullfighters retrieved the bull rope from the ground and walked over to return it to him. Saying thanks, Mustang reached for it with his gloved, left hand.

Frowning, the bullfighter stared down at Mustang's extended limb. "Hey, your arm looks kinda funny. You better have Doc Tandy look it over."

Glancing down, Mustang had to agree. It looked like he'd swallowed a tennis ball and it had gotten stuck in his arm. "I will. Thanks, man."

He grabbed the rope with his right hand and headed behind the chutes, wondering what the hell could have happened to his muscle during a damn near-perfect ride.

The first indication something was wrong was the stone-faced sports medicine team that surrounded him, followed closely by the worried expression on Slade's face as he walked up behind them and joined the group staring at Mustang's arm.

Oh yeah, and then there was the fact his limb was rapidly blowing up like a balloon. It was starting to look a lot like Popeye's famed forearm, without the anchor tattoo.

The idea that maybe he should consider getting a tattoo skidded into his mind from out of nowhere. That errant thought was quelled as his stomach began to feel a little queasy.

"Sit down, Mustang." Doc Tandy put a hand on Mustang's shoulder.

"I don't need to sit down. I'm fine. I just pulled a muscle in my arm is all."

Someone slid the nearest chair beneath his ass and he was pushed down into it in spite of his protest. Doc Tandy whipped out a penlight and shined it into Mustang's eyes.

"What are you doing? I didn't hit my head." He squinted at the doctor until an assistant came at his shirtsleeve with a scissor. Then all his attention was on her. She slipped the metal blades under the rolled sleeve just below his elbow and he heard the material give way with a tear. "Hey. You cut my shirt."

Doc Tandy shook his head. "Mustang, I'm a hell of a lot more concerned about your arm than your sleeve. You can buy a new shirt."

Slade squatted down in front of Mustang's chair. "You okay, man?"

"Besides the fact I need a new shirt? Yeah. Why?" Why was everyone acting like there was something wrong with him?

"Because your face is as white as the bed sheets in the trailer. Besides that, I know you haven't even looked up at your score yet because if you had you'd be bragging to me about it." .

"Sure I looked." Didn't he see his score on the monitor? He

must have.

"Oh yeah? What was it?" Slade pursed his lips and waited.

Mustang frowned, damned if he could remember what it had been, if he had seen it to begin with.

"He's getting shocky from the break." The doctor spoke directly to Slade as if Mustang wasn't there.

"Break? What break? Nothing's broke." Mustang started to stand up and was promptly pushed back down by more than one hand.

The doctor's face appeared in front of him right next to Slade's. "Your arm's broke."

Mustang shook his head. "No, it's not. It doesn't even hurt."

"It will when that adrenaline wears off. Adrenaline is a powerful drug, son." The doctor probed at the swollen forearm.

It hadn't hurt before, but it sure as hell was starting to now that the doc was messing with it. Mustang wiped the moisture from his forehead with the shirtsleeve on his good arm, wondering why he was sweating when he felt so cold. "It's fine. I just strained a muscle or something. Right, doc?"

The doctor's head swayed slowly back and forth. "No, Mustang. I'm afraid not. It's broken for sure. We need to get you to the hospital for X-rays to see how bad, but I wouldn't be surprised if it needed surgery."

Broken. Surgery. The words hit Mustang like a sledgehammer blow to the head. "My arm can't be broken. I didn't even hit the ground. You can't break a bone just from riding."

Chase Reese must have wandered over at some point, but Mustang didn't notice until he started talking. "You sure can. I saw it happen to a guy while I was riding in the college rodeo."

Mustang frowned, finding it harder than it should have

been to focus on what Chase was saying. "You went to college?"

"Yup. I even graduated." Chase grinned.

"Huh." For some reason Mustang found that fact particularly amazing, more so even than the possibility he'd gotten hurt without falling off the bull. The throbbing in his arm began to increase and he found he was having trouble comprehending much of anything.

Chase continued. "Anyway, the bull bucked so hard, it snapped this guy's arm. He didn't even notice until the ride was over."

Mustang glanced down at his own sleeveless limb again. The strange lump in the middle of his forearm was less obvious now that the whole thing had blown up to a good three times its normal size.

"Okay. Maybe it is a slight break. We'll go to the hospital. The doc will set it right quick, then I'll be back in competition in a few weeks."

Doc Tandy shook his head once more. Mustang was starting to get pretty tired of that. "You're out for at least three, maybe four months."

Chase nodded vigorously. "Yup. That's about how long that other guy was out when it happened to him. He missed the whole end of the season."

Mustang resisted the urge to punch the young rider in the face for that news. *Four months.* That would take him out of competition until the fall. He'd have barely two months to ride before the finals and the end of the season.

"Nah, I won't be out that long. I heal real fast. Right, Slade? I'll be back in eight weeks. Tops." Somehow, Mustang thought counting his time off the circuit in weeks rather than months would make it sound like less. He'd been wrong.

Slade shook his head. "Mustang, you'll heal, but it'll take some time. You should be grateful it's not worse. Listen to the doc. Don't push it."

Easy for Slade to be calm. It wasn't his damn career or paycheck on the line. Maybe Slade was just afraid of a little competition for the world title.

Everyone seemed to be siding against him, even the doctor.

"You'll be healthy enough to do plenty of other things while your arm's mending. But you can't get on a bull, not in competition and not at home, before it's totally healed."

The rules on the pro circuit said the doctor's decision was final. If he said a rider couldn't compete, that was it.

Mustang had to change the doctor's mind. "But I could—"

"Jeez, man. It's your riding arm. You know the kind of beating that arm takes during a ride." Slade's gaze dropped pointedly to Mustang's balloon-like limb.

"You can't ride, Mustang. You'll only snap it again worse and maybe next time we won't be able to fix it. Do you want to be out for good? You ready to retire at twenty-something years old? Because that's what's gonna happen if you get on a bull with that arm before it's ready." Why did the doctor suddenly sound a lot like Mustang's father when he'd lectured him as a child?

"I'll ride right-handed." Yeah. That was perfect.

"You can do that?" Chase's eyes opened wide with wonder. The younger guys were so easy to impress.

"No, he can't." Slade sneered.

"I could try."

Slade let out a sigh. "You'll only get yourself hurt worse when you fall off. Christ, Mustang. Just take the damn time off. Give yourself a chance to heal. Come back healthy so you'll still have a career to come back to."

"This is bullshit, Slade. You know you'd be on a bull again next week if it was you, hurt or not." As the pain shot through him with every beat of his pulse, Mustang found his temper growing shorter.

"No. Maybe that might have been true a few years ago when I was young and stupid, but not now."

What had suddenly made Slade all mature and conservative? Probably dating Jenna. Mustang scowled. If love made a man a weak sissy, like the way Slade was acting now, then Mustang wanted nothing to do with it.

The doctor interrupted Mustang's ponderings on love. "Listen to your friend, Mustang."

He didn't want to listen and he wasn't considering Slade a friend now that he was siding against him. It was Mustang's arm and his body. He knew it best.

Doc Tandy watched Mustang's face throughout his silent protest. "Look, we *really* need to get you to the hospital for X-rays."

He was about to agree, if only to get the damn X-rays to prove the old doctor wrong, when Chase spoke up, "Um, Slade. Security seems to have Jenna in custody."

"What?" Slade's head whipped around.

Mustang raised his eyes. Jenna was indeed in the midst of an argument with not one, but two security officers who'd dared to stop her while she was trying to get behind the chutes to where he sat.

She pointed at them now. "Look, he's right there. I just want to make sure he's okay."

Slade let out a big sigh and stood up. "I better go straighten this out before someone ends up bloody or in jail."

If he knew Jenna and her New York attitude at all, Mustang had a feeling it would be the guards who ended up bloody and Jenna in jail. Mustang grinned for the first time since getting the news Ballbreaker had broken is arm.

"Mustang. Hospital. Now." The doctor delivered the order with clipped, stern words that left no room for argument.

Inexplicably giddy—maybe he was going into shock—Mustang nodded. "Okay, doc. Am I driving, or do you want to?"

Doc Tandy raised a brow. "Funny man. Let's go."

Chapter Two

"Umm...Miss Beckett?"

Sage glanced up from the glue-covered table she'd been trying to clean before any more little sticky fingers got into it. In front of her stood a trembling five-year-old. "Yes, June?"

"I...I..." The girl's quivering turned into sobs. A closer look at the wet spot in the crotch of June's pants revealed the cause.

Sage glanced up and caught the eye of Mrs. Ross. The teacher sat, picture book in hand, in the center of a circle of children.

"I'll be right back," Sage mouthed silently.

Mrs. Ross nodded and continued to read aloud to the group.

"Come on, sweetie. We can take care of that." Taking the child by the shoulder, Sage steered her toward the door. She paused only momentarily on their trip to the girl's bathroom to stop at her desk.

Sage grabbed a pair of tiny new panties from the bottom drawer. "We'll take care of this and no one will know a thing. It'll be our little secret. All right?"

The preschooler nodded, still shakily gasping for breath between sobs.

A few minutes later, Sage held the damp crotch of June's

jeans in front of the hot air blowing out of the electric hand dryer. The impatiently waiting June danced from foot to foot in her new undies.

Sage smiled indulgently. "Just another minute, honey."

June nodded and moved on to walking in circles as she waited. A minute to a preschooler might as well be an hour. Sage held the pants closer to the air dispenser and wished the fabric dry as the cell phone in her own pants pocket vibrated.

Just another day in the life and training of a student preschool teacher.

She managed to grab the phone one-handed and glanced at the caller ID. It was her sister, who should have known she'd be at work. Sage would call her back later when she didn't literally have her hands full. She could only indulge one person at a time. Rosemary would have to wait her turn.

With another glance at June, who had just about run out of patience waiting for her pants to dry, Sage sighed. She held the garment up for another evaluation. The fabric felt damp but was dry enough the spot wouldn't be noticeable. That would have to do because from the looks of her, June was ready to sprint back to the classroom in nothing but her T-shirt, sneakers and her little pink underwear.

"Good enough. Come here, sweetie."

The child's eyes lit up at the indication she'd soon be released from her tiled prison. Sage bent down and held the pants close to the floor. June braced herself with one tiny hand on each of Sage's shoulders and stepped into the jeans. One quick tug up, a zip and a snap and she was dressed and ready to go, and go she did.

Sage laughed as the girl ran back into the classroom and took her spot in the story circle as if nothing had ever happened. If only adults could bounce back from things that quickly.

The large clock on the wall told Sage there was half an hour before parents would start arriving for afternoon pickup. Meanwhile, rapidly hardening globs of white glue waited to be scraped up, toys needed to be returned to their plastic bins and, since it was an unseasonably cool day, every one of the kids would need help donning and zipping their spring jackets as their rides home arrived.

At some point, she would also have to call her sister back or bear the wrath. Rosemary would never understand how busy Sage's life could get. Her world and her problems could never equal Rosemary's, according to Rosemary anyway.

While moving a stack of papers where the students had been practicing their letters, Sage remembered she had her own schoolwork to do for her college courses when she got home, followed by a date that evening.

A date. Sage's stomach fluttered at the thought. She was meeting Jeremy after school for an early movie. She'd had no reason to say no when he'd asked. He was nice enough and she hadn't been out socially in forever, as her married sister kept reminding her.

She hated first dates, not that she went on a whole lot of them. A dull feeling of dread rather than anticipation engulfed her as she went back to tackling the messy table.

Sage finished cleaning the side she'd been working on before June's accident and moved to the other side. It was still covered with the newspaper that had failed to protect the tabletop as well as they'd hoped it would. As she began folding the large sheets in an attempt to contain the mess, a single photo stopped her dead. It was splattered with glue and sprinkled with glitter, but she could still make out quite clearly the figure on the sports page. She knew who it would be about without even reading the caption. A glutton for punishment, she read it anyway.

Local bull rider Mustang Jackson's hot streak continues as the tour heads for Trenton, New Jersey.

Sage let out a snort. Mustang hadn't been back to his home town for more than a few days here and there since he'd graduated high school and started riding pro. Yet the town paper still called him a "local" and treated him like the prodigal son. Obviously this town loved him more than he loved this town.

What sucked most was that just the sight of his name had her heart racing. Scowling at her own foolish heart, Sage crumpled the papers. With an old butter knife and a renewed and perhaps bit-too-enthusiastic vigor, she attacked the mess and pushed all thoughts of Mustang aside.

Later that night, after an uninspiring but perfectly nice date, Sage hung her purse and jacket on the hook behind the kitchen door. She had every intention of grabbing a glass of water and heading directly to bed when she heard the sound of the television.

She found her grandmother in her usual chair in the living room. "Hey, Grams. What are you still doing up?"

Her grandmother's eyes flew open wide behind her glasses as she clutched one hand to her heart. "*Mija.* You scared me nearly to death."

"Sorry. I didn't realize you were sleeping." *Or that anyone could sleep with the television on that loudly.* Sage leaned down to plant a kiss on the cheek of the woman who'd raised her and her sister since their parents' deaths in a car crash so many years ago.

Grams reached for the remote control and turned down the volume. "How was your date with Jeremy?"

"Eh. Fine. Were you waiting up for me?" Her grandmother never waited up for her. Though, truth be told, Sage hadn't been out late enough times to base a pattern of behavior on.

Patterns of behavior. Listen to her. Her college psych class was starting to get to her. Sage needed a break. Good thing the semester was over soon.

"Yes, I waited up. I knew you'd want to hear this. I was talking to Myra Jackson. Michael got hurt riding one of his bulls."

Sage felt the world close in around her. She gripped the back of her grandmother's recliner. "How badly is he hurt?"

Her grandmother shrugged. "I'm not sure, *mija*, but Myra said he's going to need surgery."

Surgery. Oh God. Sage swallowed hard.

Visions of emergency helicopters swooping down upon the arena to save Mustang's life after a devastating fall from some monstrous bull filled Sage's head. Where had he been riding? The paper said Trenton, New Jersey. Was that competition this weekend? How old was that edition?

"All Myra knew was what Michael told her on the phone. That he'd broken something and was going to need surgery. She didn't have any other details." Her grandmother, a true gossip at heart, looked disappointed at Myra's shoddy information.

Sage drew in a deep, shaky breath. At least he'd been well enough to make the phone call himself. He must be okay. Maybe she could find more details on the Internet. "Thanks for telling me, Grams. If you hear anything else, you be sure to let me know. Okay?"

"I will, *mija*. Don't worry. I hope Myra has more information the next time she calls. It will be nice to have him back home again though. It's been too long since he visited last."

That was something Sage hadn't considered when she'd heard the news. Mustang was coming home. Of course, if he couldn't compete he'd come home and for more than just a few days too. Where else would he go?

"It has been a long time, Grams." But not long enough for her to forget her childhood crush on him.

"This place was much more exciting when Michael was around. He was always popping in and out visiting. Eating all my food. I like seeing a boy with a good appetite."

Mustang home again. In her grandmother's kitchen eating her food. All while Rosemary was living an hour away with her husband Bobby and their daughter. Sage's traitorous heart kicked into high gear at the thought.

"You better get in the habit of calling him Mustang, Grams. Last time he was home, he didn't take too kindly to being called Michael." Suddenly, Sage felt lighter. She even giggled at the image of what Mustang's face would look like when her grandmother called him Michael.

Her grandmother hoisted herself out of her chair. "I've called him Michael since the day he was born. I'm too old to go changing now."

If anyone could get away with calling him by his given name, Maria Juanita Consuelos could.

Mustang. Here. Again. "I'm going to bed."

"Good night, *mija*. Sleep well."

With Mustang on her mind? Doubtful. She'd never shake the growing anticipation within her enough to rest tonight. "Thanks, Grams. You too."

Chapter Three

"At least it's only a broken arm," Jenna pointed out while Slade opened the hotel room door.

Mustang dragged in slowly behind the pair. He was exhausted. First he'd suffered through the long painful trip to the hospital where he'd felt each bump in the road vibrate through his broken arm. Then whatever had been in the injection the doctor had given him for the pain once he'd gotten there had made him sleepy.

Slade sent a look of shock in Jenna's direction. "It's his riding arm."

Given his state at the moment, Mustang was going to skip explaining to Jenna that a bull rider having *just a broken arm* was pretty bad when it was the arm he used to stay on the bull. As it turned out, he didn't have to say anything because Slade had.

A frown furrowed her brow. "What does that mean?"

Mustang couldn't blame a city girl like Jenna for not realizing the ramifications of his injury. Compared to how she'd watched Slade get dragged around and trampled by Ballbreaker in Tulsa, Mustang's perfectly beautiful eight-second ride and dismount must have looked like a ballet to her.

How he'd managed to break his ulna, as the doctor had informed him the mangled bone was officially called, probably baffled Jenna as much as it did Mustang. "It means I'm out of competition. I can't ride again for most of the season."

"Oh. I'm so sorry, Mustang." She did appear almost as crushed as he felt as she walked over and wrapped her arms around his waist gently.

He laughed. Didn't it figure? *Now* she wanted to get affectionate. He could have used this interest last night when he'd gone to bed horny and alone. "It's not your fault, darlin'."

Glancing at Slade's unhappy face, Mustang squeezed Jenna with his good arm and then released her. "I'm just gonna shower and then get out of your way here."

Jenna reached out and touched his good arm. "I don't think you should be alone tonight."

"I'm fine. Really. Whatever the doctor gave me did the trick. I'll just shower and go to the trailer. I'm about to crash." Right now, he'd be happy with hot water on his tired muscles and a soft pillow beneath his head. He could worry about how to come up with three to four months worth of living expenses and payments on the trailer in the morning.

Jenna drew in a sharp breath and pushed the sleeve of her shirt back from her watch. "That reminds me. You need to take a pain pill."

She scurried for the small white paper bag they'd picked up from the hospital pharmacy. "Slade, can you get him some water from the bathroom?"

Mustang shook his head. "Jenna. Stop. I don't think I want to take any of those pills right now."

Jenna's eyes opened wide. "What do you mean? You have to. The doctor said the break was almost a compound fracture. If it had been any worse, the broken bone would have poked right out through your skin."

That was an image Mustang didn't need filling his brain. *Thank you, Jenna.* Her and her vivid powers of description.

More devastating was the severity of the break wasn't the worst news the doctor had delivered. He'd also said the bone had twisted, not just broken. Mustang had to have an operation to put a metal plate and screws in his forearm or never ride again. The orthopedic surgeon couldn't do the surgery that night. In fact, he wouldn't be able to fit him into the schedule for a few days, so they had wrapped his arm like a mummy, handed him some pills and a sling, and sent him on his way.

Luckily, Mustang's brain was so fuzzy from being pumped full of painkillers he didn't really care too much he couldn't get the operation taken care of right away.

As Jenna moved toward him while struggling with the childproof bottle cap, Mustang ran his right hand along the back of his neck. The meds the emergency-room doc had given him had really done a number on him. He couldn't imagine adding anything more on top of them just yet. "Not right now, Jenna. I'll be fine. I can take them later tonight if the pain gets too bad."

Jenna shook her head so vigorously a piece of hair fell out of her ponytail to land in front of one eye. "But the doctor said not to let the pain medication wear off. He said take the pills as prescribed."

Mustang sighed, glancing at Slade. "She always like this?"

Slade laughed. "Yeah. Pretty much."

"I'm gonna shower." Mustang reached for his buttons and was about to head for the bathroom when Jenna was suddenly in front of him, helping him out of his sling and unbuttoning his shirt.

The shirt would have to go into the garbage anyway since it now had only one sleeve, so it didn't even matter if he pulled a

35

few buttons off by accident. If he wasn't going to have sex with a woman he'd rather she not undress him, but he was in too much shock over the whole broken arm to bother fighting her.

Once his shirt was off, she gently slipped the sling back over his arm and glanced up at him. "Can you handle getting out of the rest of your clothes on your own?"

"Yeah, I'm good. Thanks, though."

Slade let out a snort. "Don't worry. If she tries to follow you into the bathroom, I'll stop her."

"Well, now. Let's not get too hasty." Mustang grinned.

Jenna rolled her eyes. "I guess the painkillers haven't affected you too badly."

"Nope. I'm sure I could muster up the energy for..." Mustang halted halfway through his bawdy joking when Jenna crossed the room and started rummaging through the trash. "What in the hell are you doing, woman?"

Pulling the half-full garbage bag out of the trashcan, she fished around in the bottom and emerged with a folded plastic bag and a triumphant smile.

"It's to cover your sling in the shower. I've noticed in my travels that hotel housekeeping usually leaves spare bags in the bottom of the pail. See. We can cover you up so it doesn't get wet." Jenna approached him and stretched the bag over the sling and the ace bandage-swaddled arm within it. She stood on tiptoe to tie it around his neck.

Mustang grabbed her hand and began to think it was a definite possibility she might follow him into the shower and not for any reason he'd enjoy. She was starting to remind him of his mother and if that didn't dampen a man's sexual fantasy, nothing would.

"Jenna. I'll just take the sling and bandages off." He started to tug at the plastic knot around his neck with his good hand.

"No. You're not supposed to unwrap your arm. Wait, Mustang. This will work."

"Jenna." Slade walked over. "Leave the man alone."

"But..."

Slade's warning glance silenced her, but she didn't look happy. Mustang felt bad and left the damn plastic on the way she'd tied it, but decided to take the opportunity to flee while Jenna was occupied getting reprimanded.

"Slade, can I borrow a shirt?"

"Sure. They're hanging right in the closet."

Mustang pulled a shirt off a hanger and escaped into the bathroom. He closed the door behind him and flipped on the shower hot and at full force. While the room filled with steam and he struggled to get the rest of his clothes off one-handed, the reality of the situation hit him hard.

Three months off the circuit. Possibly four.

Even if money weren't an issue, which it kind of was, what the hell would he do with himself for all that time? If Mustang Jackson wasn't a bull rider, then who and what was he?

Mustang stepped beneath the spray and let the water hit him full in the face, hoping it would wash away all of the horrible things that had happened today. It didn't, but he felt a little better being clean at least.

He finished up in the shower as best he could and turned off the water. Since his right arm was just fine, he could have *finished off* something else too, like he usually did in the shower after competitions when he didn't bring a woman home, but he wasn't in the mood. He found that realization almost as scary as being out of competition for half the season.

Getting toweled off and dressed took longer than it

normally did given his new handicap. The steam in the bathroom had begun to clear by the time Mustang was clothed, but even so, a burst of cooler air from the bedroom hit him when he opened the door.

Mustang padded barefoot into the room, his boots and socks held in one hand. He figured he'd better sit down in a real chair and not try to balance on the closed toilet seat to put those on one-handed.

He found Slade alone, lying on the bed, his head supported by his arms as he watched the television. Mustang glanced around the room.

"Where's Jenna?"

"I sent her downstairs to get you snacks from the vending machine."

"Why'd you do that?"

"Because she needed something to do to make her feel useful or she probably would have been in there washing your ass for you, that's why."

"Well, as I said before..." Mustang laughed at the warning written all over Slade's face. "Just kidding. Not sure I'm up for that right now anyway."

Slade's expression showed his doubt. Mustang couldn't blame him. There had never been a time that Mustang wasn't up for *that*.

"So what are you going to do now?"

Mustang shrugged. "I'm gonna go crash in the trailer."

"I didn't mean tonight. I'm talking about the rest of the season."

"Yeah, I know what you meant. I was trying not to think about it." Mustang hooked his sock on his big toe and used his right hand to wiggle it over the rest of this foot.

"You need to get that surgery, Mustang."

"I know. I will." Mustang let his eyes focus on the stupid show on the TV screen, hoping the laugh track on the sitcom would make his own situation seem less bad.

"You going home to your parents' place? You can have the operation performed in Texas and recuperate there."

Mustang groaned. He hated the thought of crawling home hurt to his parents. "I don't know. Maybe I should have the surgery here in New Jersey. I could recuperate in the trailer. You know. Follow the circuit. Watch you and the other guys ride. You could cover the driving for a while after the operation."

Slade made a face. "Why in the world would you want to do that? Spend all that time on the road. Waste all that money on gas. All for nothing. Why don't you go home, rest and try to enjoy the time off?"

His parents, or rather his father in particular, had been against him riding in the first place. He couldn't show up now to lick his wounds. Mustang scowled. "You don't understand."

"Yeah, I do. You're too damn proud."

"No. That's not it." *Not totally, anyway.* Mustang sighed. Slade was right about one thing. He didn't have the funds to waste crisscrossing the country in the trailer if he wasn't making any income from it. Living on the road cost money. "It doesn't matter anyway. I can't follow the circuit. I'm gonna need to find work to make the payments on the trailer."

Slade sat up and leaned forward, frowning. "What did you do with all the money you won over the last few years?"

Mustang scowled. "Your ass has been riding in it for the past year."

"You sunk all of your savings into buying that trailer?"

"Not all of it. I spent a few weeks in Vegas during the last break. Didn't exactly do so good at the tables. But the down payment on the trailer wiped out most of my savings account. I figured I was still winning steady and could make more. More than enough to cover the payments and the usual living expenses."

Women. Beer. Fast food. Then of course there was gas, tolls, the occasional hotel room or airplane flight. Health insurance—thank God for that.

"Spending everything you had on a trailer was pretty poor planning. Don't you think?"

"I'm not like you, Slade. Saving all your money, settling down with one woman. I'm a spender and I'm definitely not a settler. And if I want a lecture, I can go home to my father."

Slade sighed deeply. "Look, I have plenty of money saved and you're right. I've been riding around with you for a year now. Let me cover the payments while you're out."

"No, no way." Mustang shook his head to leave no doubt in Slade's mind how adamantly opposed he was to that suggestion.

Slade frowned. "Why not?"

"I don't take handouts." Mustang shoved one foot, then the other, into his boots, ready to get out of there.

"It's not a handout. It's payment for past services rendered."

"You pay for half the gas and tolls. You paid for more than half of the oil changes, I think. So no. You're paid up."

"A loan then. You can pay me back when you're back and riding again this fall."

"No." Mustang rose just as the door opened and Jenna stepped in.

"I got you some cheese puffs and potato chips. Oh, and

chocolate chip cookies in case you wanted something sweet." She unloaded an armful of snacks onto the table. "Did you take your pain pill yet?"

How could a man stay pissed off in the face of all that sweetness? Mustang couldn't control the smile that crossed his lips. "No, ma'am. Not yet."

"Wait right there." She shot Slade a look on her way to the bathroom. "I told you to make sure he took it as soon as he got out of the shower."

"Sorry," Slade grumbled.

Mustang drew in a deep breath and planted his ass back in the chair. Slade was a friend. A good one. So was Jenna. They cared about him. He waited until she disappeared into the bathroom and he heard the water running in the sink. "Okay. I'll agree to go home for the operation and stay there while I recuperate. I should be able to find work locally for a few months."

"All right and if you can't work—"

"I'll consider your offer of a loan. Maybe."

Slade nodded. "Good enough."

It looked like Mustang was heading home for the first time in a long time. God help him.

"Magnolia, Texas, here I come." Damn. He needed a drink. Mustang raised his voice so Jenna could hear him in the bathroom. "Hey, darlin'? Do those pills say anything about taking them with liquor?"

"Mustang Jackson, you can not mix alcohol with painkillers." There was that tone again. Jenna was going to make an excellent mother to Slade's children one day.

Jenna's medical opinion or not, Mustang took the pill she forced on him and then made his escape. He left the hotel and crossed the street in search of alcohol to sooth the feeling of dread he'd had since deciding to go home.

He pushed open the door of the bar with his one arm that was sling-free, hoping for both liquor and entertainment to get his mind off his injury. He wasn't at all surprised to see the room packed with bull riders, as well as women of all ages. Cowboys appealed to females both young and old.

Apparently injured cowboys were even more attractive than the everyday variety. Mustang realized every feminine gaze in the place stayed trained on him as he made his way over to where Chase and a few of the other guys stood.

"Hey, Mustang. What'd they say at the hospital?" Chase's eyes focused on the sling.

"I'm gonna need a metal plate and a few screws...and a beer." He signaled the bartender, pointing at Chase's longneck bottle and holding up one finger.

Considering all the choices of alcohol he could mix with the pain pill Jenna had forced on him, beer seemed the most harmless. He probably hadn't needed that pill anyway, but Jenna had been relentless.

"Damn. A plate and screws. I'm sorry, man. That really sucks." His young brow furrowed beneath his blond curls.

"Yeah, tell me about it." Why was that beer taking so long? Mustang spied the bartender at the cash register ringing up another customer and sighed. Ever since he'd called his parents from the payphone in the hotel lobby and told them he was coming home, he'd really needed a drink.

"Did they tell you how long that'll keep you out for?"

"They said pretty much what Doc Tandy did. Three to four months." Mustang wished again the bartender would hurry.

Finally, the man delivered the blessed bottle of brew.

Mustang managed to get his wallet out of his pocket, but pulling out a bill one-handed was going to be a challenge.

"Here. Take that out of here." Chase pushed the pile of cash that was sitting in front of him toward the bartender.

"Thanks, kid." Mustang shoved his wallet back into his pocket and sucked down a long swallow of beer. The cold foam slid down his throat.

Chase saluted Mustang with his own bottle and a grin. "No problem. Anytime. Besides, I scored really well tonight so I'm celebrating."

"Congratulations." Mustang took another swallow and then set his bottle down, sorry his own misery made it impossible to be happy for Chase and his high score.

Noticing a small white card lying on the wood, he picked it up and read aloud. "*Guy Little. Sports Photographer.* What the hell is this?"

"Oh, yeah. You missed it. This guy—ha, that's funny since his name is Guy—anyway, he came in and gave us all cards along with some shit about us earning hundreds of bucks an hour modeling for him."

"Hundreds of bucks an hour, huh?" Mustang knew some models got paid real big bucks, but these guys were bull riders, not models. "Upfront?"

Chase nodded his head. "Yup. Supposedly he would take the pictures for some sports website that's being developed right now. He'd pay you now but the site wouldn't be up and live until later in the year."

Mustang glanced down at the card again, his mind working. "Do you want this?"

Laughing, Chase shook his head. "No. Do you?"

"Um." Mustang held the business card between two fingers.

He couldn't tell Chase he was actually considering it to make money while he was laid up. Tough Texan bull riders like himself simply didn't do things like model. Then an idea hit him. "The practical joke potential of this little baby is limitless. I can tell Slade that while he was holed up in the hotel room with Jenna, I got hired as a big-time model."

"Hey, I never thought of that." Admiration crossed Chase's face, followed closely by a devilish look. "You could even *accidentally* whip it out in front of a girl and say 'What's that? Oh, yeah. I'm a model'. You know, to impress her."

"Sure could. Good thinking, kid." His modeling aspirations to pay his bills were still a secret and Chase was learning how to be devious. Things were good. Mustang happily shoved the card into his pocket.

"So what are you going to do now?"

That seemed to be the question of the night. Mustang looked up to find Chase watching him with concern. The last thing he wanted was pity. He forced a smile.

"First, I'm gonna find me a woman and get laid. An injury is like a magnet for chicks, especially on the night it happens. Gotta take advantage of it while I can."

Shaking his head, Chase broke into an awed grin. "You are the master, Mustang. I bow to you, man."

"Stick with me, kid and I'll teach you all I know." His smile was genuine now.

Glancing around the bar and looking for likely candidates, Mustang noticed Chase's two friends. Garret and Skeeter seemed to be trying for a pair of hot girls who looked like they'd rather be elsewhere. He shook his head. "Didn't those two learn their lesson about picking up girls out of their league yet?"

Chase leaned back against the bar and laughed. "Guess not. It's fine with me if they get shot down again. We're all sharing one room. If they hook up, I'm out in the cold, or sleeping in the bathtub tonight. So which woman are you gonna go for?"

Mustang took a sip and browsed the many choices. Taking a young rider under his wing and teaching him the art of seduction was bringing back the thrill that had been missing for him lately. He nearly forgot about his arm, but not quite.

"You tell me, kid. If you could have any woman in here, which one would you want?"

"That's easy. I picked her out the minute she walked in the door. Actually, I spotted her in the stands back at the arena." Chase's gaze skipped directly to a table in the corner where a mature brunette was seated next to a man. She looked a good fifteen years older than Chase.

The kid really did stick to the same type. This woman looked a lot like Jenna. It was no secret Chase had a huge crush on her back in Tulsa.

Mustang swallowed another mouthful of beer. "So why are you way the hell over here and not over there talking to her?"

Chase's eyebrows shot up to his hairline. "Because she's here with a guy."

"Yeah, so?"

"Are you crazy? You can't hit on a woman in front of her boyfriend."

"Well, no you shouldn't do that. In that case, you wait for her boyfriend to go take a piss and then you hit on her while he's gone." Mustang observed the couple's interaction with each other and became even more convinced they weren't a couple at all. "Those two aren't dating."

Chase's eyes narrowed as he watched them across the room. "How can you tell?"

"See the way the woman's looking all around the bar but hardly ever at him? And look at how the guy is checking out the ass on that young thing playing pool. No man would do that in front of his girl unless he's looking for a fight."

Then, as if on cue, the woman noticed Mustang staring and their gazes locked. She finally broke eye contact first, but not before Mustang saw her interest. "Oh, yeah. She's available."

"But the guy—"

Mustang shook his head. "Don't worry about him. If she is with him, she doesn't want to be, but I'm telling you they're not a couple. Look. He's getting up. Come on."

"What?" Chase's voice rose to the level of a prepubescent squeak.

"We're going over there to talk to her." Mustang planted his bottle down on the wooden bar with a determined thud.

"What if he comes back and beats the crap out of us for talking to his girl? You only have one arm to fight with."

Heading across the room with Chase scurrying behind him complaining all the way, Mustang shot a disgusted look over his shoulder. "You get the shit beat out of you every week by a two-thousand-pound bull and you're worried about one guy? Man up, Chase, or you'll never get laid."

"Hey, I do okay for myself in the female department."

"Yeah, yeah. Just hush up and follow my lead."

One glance at Chase's expression told Mustang that though Chase wasn't happy, he'd at least do as he was told. With the kid under control, Mustang centered his attention on the woman. "Hey there. Did I see you in the stands while I was riding at the arena tonight? I never forget a beautiful lady. I'm Mustang Jackson, by the way."

She didn't melt at the compliment the way he'd hoped, but

she didn't shut him down either.

"Yeah, I know who you are. I was there tonight. How's the arm?"

Mustang shrugged off the injury. "Eh. Just a broken bone."

She raised a brow and laughed. "*Just* a broken bone?"

Judging by the sound of her, she was a local. In his past experience, New Jersey girls were naturally wild. This one having a bit of age on her would probably make her even more so.

Through the harsh shell of her exterior, undeniable heat radiated off this woman. The usual anticipation he always felt right before sex fluttered in his chest.

"Yeah. It's nothing. I've had worse." Mustang reached back and grabbed Chase's shoulder, pulling him forward. "This here is the reigning Rookie of the Year, Chase Reese."

"I know who he is too. I saw his win on television last year. Congratulations on Rookie of the Year."

As Chase sputtered out something that could have been thanks, her chocolate-brown gaze traveled from Chase back to Mustang and settled there.

Oh yeah. Mustang began to formulate a plan for Chase's further education in women. "What's your name, darlin'?"

"Marla." Her smile widened and turned into a chuckle.

Mustang smiled himself. "What's so amusing?"

"We don't hear men say *darlin'* up here in New Jersey too often."

If she liked that, he could definitely come up with more Texan speak for her while he was buried inside her hot, New Jersey pussy.

Chase's elbow poked into Mustang's side hard. He frowned at the kid, who was too busy staring at something across the room to notice. Mustang glanced over his shoulder and saw Marla's male companion coming out of the men's room.

No matter. Mustang proceeded as planned.

"Can we buy you a drink, darlin'?" Chase's eyes opened wide at that and Mustang decided he better deal with the situation before the kid's head exploded. "Your boyfriend over there won't mind, will he?"

She smiled. "He's not my boyfriend. He's just a friend I dragged with me so I didn't have to come alone."

Bingo. Mustang's cock stirred in his pants. He shot Chase an I-told-you-so look and went back to work. "Did you two come in separate cars?"

Her eyes narrowed with what could only be labeled as horniness. "We did."

Mustang glanced pointedly around the room. "You know, I really hate crowded, noisy bars. My trailer is parked in the lot next door. It's nice and quiet and I've got cold beer and good whisky. Would you like to join Chase and me over there for a drink?" *Or a three way?*

She hesitated and, for the briefest of seconds, Mustang thought he maybe had moved too fast.

"Sure. Just let me tell my friend I'm leaving." She stood up and walked to where her companion was already flirting with the girls at the pool table. He wouldn't object to being rid of her any more than Mustang would to ditching him. In this particular instance, three was company, four a crowd.

Next to him, Chase choked. "Oh my God. She's really coming back to your trailer."

"Yup. Do you think you can stop acting like a virgin long enough to fuck her?"

That question caused another priceless expression to cross

Chase's face, but he still managed to protest. "I'm not a virgin."

Mustang raised one eyebrow. "If you've never had a threesome, then you might as well be."

Chase paled.

Afraid the kid might pass out at the thought, Mustang lightened up on him a little bit. "Just keep your mouth shut and do what I tell you and this will be a night you'll never forget. Trust me."

Swallowing hard, Chase nodded, just as Marla made her way back toward them.

"Here she comes. Get that deer-in-headlights look off your face and let's go."

Chapter Four

"Are you sure you'll be okay driving all the way home to Texas by yourself?"

Mustang patiently answered what had to be Jenna's tenth question regarding his getting home alone. "Yes, ma'am."

"Because we can figure something out—"

"Jenna. I'll be all right. My right arm is just fine to steer. The truck has an automatic transmission so I won't have to shift again after I put it into drive and go."

Her brow furrowed with concern. "But what if you need two hands to back up the trailer or something?"

"I promise to only drive forward. Okay?" He leaned down and kissed her on the forehead. "Now, no more worrying."

The look on her face told Mustang asking that of Jenna was probably equivalent to asking her to not breathe. He gripped Slade's hand and pumped it in a handshake. "She's going to worry anyway, isn't she?"

"Yup." Slade nodded. "Remember what we talked about. If you need any—"

Not Slade too. Mustang rolled his eyes. "I remember. I won't need any."

"But if you do," Slade prompted.

"I'll call you. Promise."

Slade's lip twisted into a doubt-filled scowl. "You'll call me, huh? Do you even have my number?"

"Yes." Jenna stepped closer. "I programmed both yours and my number into his new cell phone."

Slade's brows shot up to his hairline as he addressed Mustang. "Your new what? I thought you didn't need a cell phone."

"You weren't supposed to tell him." Mustang frowned at Jenna for outing him.

"Sorry." Jenna shrugged and didn't appear at all sorry.

With a sigh, he decided he better explain or risk a good ribbing from Slade after all the torture he'd inflicted on his friend. Though in Mustang's defense, Slade's cell phone usage had become extreme the moment he and Jenna had become a long-distance couple.

"It was under protest. Your girlfriend made me get one of those pay-as-you-go phones because she's convinced I'm going to die along the highway somewhere between New Jersey and Texas."

She planted her hands on her hips. "That's like a thousand miles. You could break down and need help or something. In this day and age it is simply archaic to not have a cell phone for emergencies. I can't believe you lived this long without one."

At this point, agreeing with her seemed like the way to go. "I know. You're right. Thank you for being concerned."

Jenna looked the happiest he'd seen her since his injury. That had been simple. He should give in and humor her more often, just like Slade usually did. Slade was no dummy after all.

While she was happy and leaving him alone, Mustang figured he better get while the getting was good. "I guess I should be heading out now. Long drive ahead."

"Did you take your pain pill?"

"Yes, ma'am. I did."

Jenna nodded, satisfied. "Good, and I checked. It's fine for you to drive while you're taking them."

Mustang shot a sidelong glance at the behemoth vehicle parked nearby. The one he'd be driving one-handed halfway across the country. "Good to know."

"I put a bottle of water in the console next to you in case you get thirsty or need to take another pill," Jenna threw in quickly as Mustang was about to turn toward the trailer.

Slade hooked an arm around her neck, probably to keep her from running over and showing Mustang exactly where in the console that water was. "Jenna. He lives in the trailer. He's got everything he needs inside."

"I know, but when he's driving he might not want to stop or there might not be anyplace to pull over."

"If that's the case he shouldn't be drinking 'cause eventually the man is gonna have to stop and take a piss from all that water." Slade kissed the top of her head as a scowl twisted her lips.

Shaking his head, Mustang opened the driver's side door but couldn't resist turning back for one last hug from Jenna. "You drive yourself safely back to New York. Okay, darlin'?"

"I will." Her eyes looked a little misty so Mustang moved on before he got choked up himself.

This was starting to feel too much like goodbye. Three or four months wasn't forever, but it sure felt like a damn long time right now.

He moved on to Slade, slapping him on the back. "You be careful in that bad-ass muscle car of yours. Don't speed too fast on the way to Baltimore because I won't be there to bail you out of jail if you get caught."

"He won't." Jenna answered with a warning glance at her boyfriend.

Slade smiled. "Don't worry about me, man. You just take care of yourself and let that arm heal."

"I will." What choice did he have?

"Call when you get home." Jenna jumped in. "Or even before you get there from the road. Okay? You have five-hundred minutes loaded on your phone to start and remember you can add more when you need to."

After he found a job, made the trailer payments and had money left over, he'd do just that, but he sure as hell wasn't borrowing money from his parents. Over his dead body.

Mustang nodded. "I remember. Thank you."

Seeing that Jenna may have possibly run out of instructions for the moment, he took the opportunity to climb into the cab of the trailer.

He slammed the door and rolled down the window. As he fired up the diesel engine, he shouted out one last goodbye. Mustang made sure he looked extra confident driving one-handed until he was out of sight of Jenna and Slade. Then he breathed a sigh.

He'd held on to the happy face for their benefit but it was going to be a long, lonely drive. He wasn't looking forward to it. The operation on his arm and recuperating with his father telling him *I told you so* for at least the next three months weren't looking too great either.

Glad Jenna the worrier wasn't there to see it, Mustang made a rather sloppy turn onto the main street, heading toward the entrance to the highway when a shiny white vehicle sped up behind the trailer.

The jacked-up, new pickup truck pulled next to him, beeping the entire way. The automatic passenger window slid smoothly down and Chase leaned across from the driver's seat. "Mustang. Hey, you taking off?"

Mustang pulled over to the side of the street, figuring he didn't need any more distractions while driving with one arm in a sling. Chase pulled in front of him, hopped out and jumped up on the running boards on the trailer's driver side.

"Hey, Chase. Yeah, I'm heading home for the surgery."

"Damn. Good luck with that."

Mustang nodded. "Thanks."

"So, last night with Marla..." Chase shook his head. "Wow. I mean that was amazing."

Mustang couldn't help but smile at the kid's enthusiasm. "Yeah, I guess it was."

Chase grinned like a little boy on Christmas morning. "I got her phone number."

Only this kid would plan on calling a woman they'd picked up at a bar for a threesome, but that was what made Chase who he was. A corn-fed, God-fearing, well-mannered, Oklahoman cowboy right down to the bone.

"Good for you, kid."

"I'm gonna wait 'til later today to call though. Don't want to look too anxious. She's probably sleeping late anyway after last night. Oh hey, are you gonna call her too? Because I mean, if you do that's fine with me."

"No, I'm good. Thanks." Mustang laughed and then glanced at the clock in the dashboard. "Anyway, I better get on the road."

"Yeah. We're all gonna miss you around here." Chase leaned in the window and hugged him. A quick, manly, one-armed hug, but more than Mustang wanted or expected from the kid. Especially after having been with him naked just hours before, even if there had been a woman in between them.

Uncomfortable with the show of affection, Mustang quickly came up with something to say. "I'll be back in a few months. It'll be like I was never gone."

If only he believed that were true.

"Yeah. Maybe we can hang out again then. After you're back." Chase looked hopeful.

"Sure. We'll see. Good luck in Baltimore."

"Thanks." Chase hopped down and, with one last wave, climbed back into his truck.

Reaching his right hand over to the left side of the steering column, Mustang flipped on his blinker. He threw the truck in drive and pulled away from the curb, but as he drove away Mustang didn't see the road in front of him. Instead, he saw his future.

He didn't like what he saw.

Slade and Jenna were already paired off and happier on their own than spending time with him. Sure, he could keep hanging out with the younger guys like Chase, until they all found themselves steady girlfriends or got married. Then what? Mustang would move on to hanging with the next set of single guys.

The older he became, the younger the new guys would get until one day he'd be a scarred, retired, former champion bull rider with a trophy case full of buckles and not much of anything else. Old. Alone. Lonely.

Suddenly being free and single and available to be with any woman he wanted on any given night wasn't so attractive. He pictured Jenna as she tied the plastic bag around his neck so he could shower. Maybe having a woman mothering him and telling him what he could and couldn't do wouldn't be so bad after all.

Depressed now, he headed down the highway jealous of everyone in the world. Slade, who was probably on his way back to the hotel room to have sweaty sex with Jenna. Chase, for being so young and starry eyed he might actually make things work with their one-night stand, Marla. And every other bull rider on the circuit because they weren't heading home to get a metal plate and screws put in their arm. Oh, no. They'd be riding in Baltimore next week while he was in hell, recovering from surgery at his parents' house.

Life really wasn't fair.

Over the next day the feeling of dread lodged in Mustang's chest increased steadily the nearer he got to the place of his birth. It peaked as he saw the sign for Huntsville, Texas.

Speeding faster than was wise past the city, he became very much aware he was following the same route his grandfather had, and his father still took, to Huntsville Prison every working day of their adult lives. Just like Mustang had been supposed to if he had bowed to his father's pressure years ago and followed in his footsteps.

Becoming a third-generation prison guard hadn't exactly been Mustang's lifelong ambition. Not that his father would ever understand Mustang's willingness to give up what was in his eyes a good, steady job with benefits to instead take a chance on making a living riding bulls, of all things.

He sent thanks up to God that he'd gotten that job at the ranch and discovered he could sit a bull, even if his decision to ride pro hadn't gone over real well at home. His father's predictions then had been that Mustang would eventually come crawling home either broke or broken.

The trailer hit a bump in the road and he felt the twinge as it jarred his arm in the sling. That served as a very real reminder that he was indeed coming home a bit broken as well as a little broke at the moment.

Mustang felt the hard bulk of his Rookie-of-the-Year belt buckle beneath his broken arm. His father hadn't been right. He had made something of himself and he had the proof right there, pressed against his gut where his self-doubt lived.

Bones healed and Mustang had no doubt that he'd be back on the circuit winning again in just a few months—if he survived living with his father that long. On that cheery thought, he pulled the trailer into the city limits of Magnolia and slowed to the local speed limit.

With the exception of the for-rent sign on what had been Hackett's Hardware during his youth, Main Street looked pretty much the same as it had the last time he'd passed through for a quick, painful visit home.

As he wound his way out of the center of town and toward the country road that led to his parents' house, Mustang saw other changes. A few large trees had fallen down. They'd uprooted actually. There'd been some nasty storms in Texas over the past year. High winds, tornados, flooding.

Stifling the guilt, he reminded himself he'd called home to check on his family after each and every bout of bad weather had passed through the area. What more could he do from the road when he had competitions nearly every week?

Occupied with justifying to himself that his long absences were unavoidable, not just his attempt to avoid his father, Mustang didn't notice the strange car parked in front of the house. He didn't see it until he'd pulled the trailer under the trees around the side and was headed on foot for the front door.

The unfamiliar white car was about the size of a toy. He

couldn't imagine either his six-foot-tall father or his generously proportioned mother picking it as their new vehicle. Mustang's father, like his father before him, was a pickup-truck man and his mama was a four-door sedan with a trunk big enough to fit a body in kind of lady.

Still wondering about the car, Mustang raised his hand to open the front door while kicking the dust off his boots on the mat. He didn't bother to knock. Doors in this house had never been locked and most likely never would be, even if they had known where the key was.

Mustang didn't have a chance to turn the knob before it was yanked from his hand and the door flung open. He suddenly had an armful of his mother. She wrapped herself around his neck while kissing his face.

"Watch the arm, Ma." He hadn't taken a pain pill in awhile. Good thing Jenna wasn't there. She'd be shoving one down his throat before he could stop her.

His mother stepped back, focusing on his sling. "Oh my God. Michael, I'm so sorry. Does it hurt?"

"Not too bad." Except for when he'd fallen asleep after his and Chase's fun with Marla without taking a pill first and had woken up in agony. He didn't mention that and instead shrugged. "I'll be fine. Good as new as soon as the doc operates."

"At least it's your left arm. Since you're right-handed, if your right arm had been out of commission I probably would've never been able to convince them to hire you at work."

At the sound of his father's voice, Mustang swung his head to locate the man. He found him lurking in the shadows to the side of the door.

"What do you mean? You got me a job at the prison?"

Dear God, if he didn't recover fully, if he couldn't ride

again, would he have to do the one thing he'd left this town to avoid? Would he be forced to follow his father and grandfather's path whether he wanted to or not?

"As soon as your surgeon says you can work, you've got a position waitin' on you at the prison. And let me tell you, it wasn't easy to get either, with your arm broken and all. I had to call in some favors."

Great, so now he was expected to owe his father for getting him a job he didn't want.

"It's nothing in the high-security areas, mind you. It's more like a glorified secretary, mostly watching monitors, filling out reports, but it's a foot in the door. It'll help when you finally come to your senses and decide it's time to grow up and get a real job."

And there it was, the expected verbal slam and it had been only—Mustang glanced at the watch on his right wrist—two minutes or so since he'd walked through the front door.

There were clearly two options here. He could tell his father to take his job offer and his attitude and shove it right up where the sun didn't shine, after which he would have to get back in the trailer. He supposed he could recuperate while parked in the lot behind the hospital. Or he could do what he always did. Keep his mouth shut and go out later. He'd find a bar and a woman, get drunk and get laid and take his mind off it all.

Mustang set his jaw. There was no way he could endure four months of this. Not even with all the booze and women in the world to help him. "I'll have to see what my plans are. I was hoping to take off as soon as the doc said it was okay for me to travel. You know, get back on the road. Join the guys on tour again."

He'd have to take Slade up on his offer of money, but it would be worth it. Swallowing his pride would be a lot easier than biting his tongue around his father for all that time. He'd likely bite his tongue damn near off by the time his bone healed.

His mother's hand touched his right arm gently. "Oh, no, Michael. I was hoping to have you around for a while this time. I miss you."

As his father turned and walked out of the room, Mustang heard, "As if he cares about anyone but himself."

Mustang tore his gaze from his father's stiff back. Leaving his mother would be his only regret when he pulled out of this damn town. "Don't worry, Ma. You'll have me around long enough to get sick of me."

His father apparently already was. He drew in a deep sigh and decided to change the subject.

"What's for dinner? I'm so hungry my stomach's eating my backbone." Mustang turned toward the kitchen and stopped dead at the sight that greeted him.

Her glossy dark brown hair hung to her shoulders and just begged for a man to tangle his hands in it. But what really caught his attention was the afternoon sun slanting through the window behind her. It outlined her long, lean, hotter-than-hell, girl-next-door body through the thin cotton of her dress.

His gaze traveled back up to her face and Mustang realized this *was* the girl next door. Or at least the girl that lived on the next street in a house where he'd spent a considerable amount of his youth, and man oh man had she grown up.

He frowned, shocked. "Little Bit?"

A shy, innocent smile lit her fresh, sweet face. "It's been a long time since I've been called that. Welcome home, Mustang."

It sure as hell had been a long time. Long enough for Rosemary's younger sister to be not so little anymore.

"Thanks. It's good to be home."

Good to be home? Had he actually just said that? Damn, he was having trouble thinking with the grownup version of Sage in the room.

"To answer your question about dinner, Sage just came to drop off Maria's empanadas especially for you." His mother's answer to his previous and long-forgotten question caught his attention.

The fact that Sage's grandmother had cooked just for him warmed his heart when he needed it most. News of her homemade empanadas would have had him jumping for joy any day. Add to that the fact Sage had come to greet him the moment he'd gotten home and he was excited in a whole other way.

The sweet, younger Beckett girl had always shown him kindness, even in the old days when she was just a kid. Then again, she'd seemed more mature mentally and emotionally than her girlish exterior indicated. She'd listen to him complain about his parents with the patience of someone much older. Far more patience than Rosemary ever displayed for anything.

He let his gaze roam over her again. Rosemary may have been the belle of Magnolia back in high school, but Sage, the quiet, nerdy late-bloomer, had far surpassed her sister. Who the hell could have guessed that the knobby-kneed, eyeglass-wearing, quiet sister would end up becoming the natural beauty in the family?

Then it hit him like a brick to the head. He couldn't think about Sage like a woman. He sure as hell couldn't treat her the way he usually treated women. Grams going to all the trouble to make him his favorite dinner only served to remind him that the youngest granddaughter of the woman who'd been like a second mother to him was off-limits, especially since he had no plans to stick around here any longer than he had to.

Mustang let out a long, deep breath to steady himself. Too often he did his thinking with his dick. This was one girl he couldn't do that with. "How is your grandmother, Sage?"

She laughed, making her look even younger than she had before, but that didn't stop the warmth that spread through him at the sound.

"Grams is the same as always." Her cheeks dimpled as she smiled.

How old would she be now? He quickly did the math, trying to remember how old she'd been when he left town those many years ago. She had to be twenty, give or take a year. Old enough, which made her far too tempting.

Yup. He needed to keep his hormones in check, but that didn't mean he couldn't catch up with an old friend. She'd always been a good listener and just as good about keeping quiet and sitting with him in silence when he hadn't been in the mood to talk.

That would be nice, having a female friend whom he'd never had sex with. It sure as hell would be new.

"You be sure to tell her how much I appreciate the food. It's been too long since I've had home cooking."

Home cooking usually required a home, which meant coming home to the hell that was his father. Until now that had been less than enticing. Taking another look at Sage, all grown up and looking fine, and imagining how good those empanadas were going to taste, Mustang was rethinking his former opinion. Maybe Magnolia did offer a few enticements after all. But shit, only one of those two things was a guilt-free pleasure he'd be able to allow himself.

His mother ran her hand up and down his good arm, yanking his attention away from the only thing he'd been able to focus on since she'd walked out of the kitchen.

"Well, you're going to get home cooking for as long as you're here."

"Thanks, Ma. That'll be nice."

"Come on. Let's sit and eat. Sage was kind enough to bring the food over still hot so it's all ready to eat. It sounds like your father is already poking around in it."

"Um, I'm gonna head home now. Good seeing you again." Sage sidled toward the door, putting her closer to Mustang.

He breathed in deeply and caught a whiff of whatever fresh, floral scent she wore. It mingled with the smell of Grams' empanadas and he couldn't resist. He wanted to keep her around for a little longer. "Why don't you stay and eat with us?"

"I couldn't impose on ya'll like that."

His mother shook her head. "Don't be silly. Maria sent enough food for half the town. We'd love for you to stay. You can catch Michael up on all the goings on with the young people in town."

"Yeah, Little Bit. Stay. Tell me everything I've missed." He definitely didn't want her to go yet and it had nothing to do with his wanting to hear what was happening in town either. The only person he wanted to hear about was Sage.

She hesitated. "Okay. I'll stay. Thanks, Mrs. Jackson."

"My pleasure, darlin'." His mother bustled off into the kitchen, but Mustang held back.

He shook his head. "You sure have grown up."

Sage cocked one dark brow.

"I'm glad you noticed." The low, sultry tone of her voice cut straight through him.

She spun and followed his mother into the kitchen. He watched her hips sway and let out a long, slow breath. Gone without a trace was any resemblance to the little girl he used to know. How the hell was he going to keep his hands off her? It damn sure wasn't going to be easy.

Chapter Five

"You really don't have to come to the hospital."

As Mustang sat and tried not to drool over the remains of breakfast left on his parents' plates, his stomach protested being empty with a big rumble. The aroma of freshly cooked bacon still hung in the air, but grumbling belly or not, there'd be no food or even water for him until after the surgery.

His mother put down her coffee mug and frowned. "Of course I'm taking you to the hospital. You're my baby and you're having an operation."

"Ma. I just turned twenty-six." He couldn't help but smile.

"I don't care how old you are. You'll always be my baby."

"Damned inconvenient to schedule surgery in the middle of the week so your mother has to take off work," his father mumbled from behind the morning paper.

Mustang drew in a deep breath to calm himself before he was tempted to use his one good arm in a way no son should think of using it against his father.

"It was the only day the surgeon could do it. Don't take off work, Ma. I'm serious. You don't need to come with me. I'll drive myself to the hospital."

"Don't be silly. It's fine. I've already called my boss and explained. They can do without me for one day. Besides, you can't drive yourself home after surgery."

An annoyed snort came from behind the paper and as stupid an idea as it was, Mustang was still tempted to drive himself. He didn't care if he had to sleep in the hospital parking lot until he was up to the trip home. His mind reeled. Maybe he could say he'd already asked a friend to drive him to the hospital. Not that he had any close friends left in Magnolia, unless he counted Sage.

Mmm. Sage. Thoughts of her sweet smile and hot little body raised his spirits, but didn't do a damn thing to solve the issue at hand.

He had walked Sage to the door after dinner. Maybe his parents might believe he'd asked her to drive him then. Though the fact that his trailer was missing when he was supposed to be in a car with Sage might be a clue he was lying, even to his dense, self-absorbed father. Maybe he could say it was parked at her house, but his mother might check with Grams.

Shit. He should have stayed in New Jersey.

"Well, time for work." His father's chair scraped back from the table. He stood and headed for the door.

Watching his father leave without another word, Mustang figured he wasn't going to get as much as a simple "good luck with the operation" or hell, a "don't die on the table because I'm not paying to bury you" from him.

The man was halfway to the door when he turned back. "Don't forget to ask the doctor when you can start work."

Mustang set his jaw. "I'll ask." *I'll ask when I can get the hell away from here.*

With a satisfied nod, he was gone.

After that beginning, the day could only get better, even with the broken bone and surgery. Just being away from his father lifted a dark cloud from Mustang's brain. The drugs they gave him at the hospital didn't hurt either.

"Michael. I'm going to give you a little something I call giggle juice when I'm talking to the kids, but it's really—" Sticking the IV needle into Mustang's right arm, the doctor spoke in that way all doctors did as they tried to make even complex things sound simple.

"That's okay. I don't need to know any more than that. Giggle juice is just fine. And call me Mustang." Feeling queasy from just looking at the needle sliding into his vein, Mustang thought it best to interrupt before he went any further with the explanation.

"That's right. The famous Mustang Jackson. We have a bit of a celebrity here with us today." He smiled and spoke to the nurse while injecting a syringe full of what Mustang guessed was the giggle juice into the IV line.

Mustang averted his gaze and tried to concentrate on the mint green walls instead of the steady drip, drip of liquid slowly filtering into his arm. Even the toughest men had their weaknesses. His was needles.

A nurse with an ass the size of Texas steered a wheelchair through the door and over to the bed. "Hop on in here, sweetie. You qualify for a free ride to the operating room."

Mustang started to protest that he could walk when he started to feel spacey. Resolved that he would be pretty much powerless to stop her and not caring so much anymore, he let the nurse help him into the chair. His IV bag full of giggle juice came along for the ride as she wheeled him through the double doors to surgery.

Time started to pass in strange ways and the next thing he knew, they were telling him to hop up onto the operating table. In a haze, he lay down, crossing his legs like he always did when he was relaxing.

"Uncross your legs, please." The anesthesiologist was less of a people person than the doctor. No joking around. Just orders.

Mustang was pretty sure he complied with the request, but couldn't be sure. He wasn't aware of another thing until he woke up in recovery, alone, starving and feeling like he'd downed a bottle of tequila.

If only that were true...

"Look who's awake. How do you feel?" The well-rounded nurse walked closer to the bed.

"Thirsty. Hungry too, I think."

"Good. We'll get you something to drink and eat as soon as the doctor sees you."

The doctor walked around the curtain right on cue. "Hey, there. Do I hear someone's hungry?"

Food would be good, but a report that he'd be back riding sooner instead of later would be even better. "Did everything go all right, doc? With the operation, I mean."

Consulting the chart at the end of the bed, the doctor nodded. "Perfect. The ulna was twisted. Basically, half of the bone did a one-hundred-and-eighty-degree turn when you broke it. We had to go in, twist it back around and then secure it with a plate. You are now the proud new owner of one metal plate and four screws, but the bone will heal just fine."

Good thing vivid visuals of snapped bones in his body didn't bother Mustang as much as needles did or that would have been way too much information. "Am I gonna set off the metal detectors at the airport now?"

Sticking his pen back into his pocket, the doctor laughed. "No. The new metal we use doesn't set off metal detectors."

Mustang's woozy brain spared a brief moment to consider why criminals didn't just get guns made out of this new metal if it didn't set off the detectors. He wrestled his focus back onto what was really important. "When do you think I'll be able to use the arm again?"

He replaced the chart at the foot of the bed. "That depends what we're talking about. As long as you're careful, I don't see why by tomorrow you couldn't do most everything you're used to doing, just with the sling on. You can drive and shower as long as you keep the bandages from getting wet."

"And when can I ride again?"

The doctor shaking his head had both Mustang's hopes and gut sinking.

"I will be able to ride again, right?"

"You will, yes. Mustang, you're not the first professional cowboy I've patched up. This is Texas, you know. I'm telling you right now, you get back on a bull before you're ready and I can make no guarantees that it won't end your career."

Mustang took a second to breathe and resolve himself to that. "Okay."

The doctor raised an eyebrow. "Does that mean you'll follow my advice or are you just going to do what you want anyway?"

"It means I'm not ready to retire." Even if that meant having to swallow his pride for the next four months. "I'll do what it takes to go back into competition one-hundred percent healthy, doc. I promise."

"Good to hear." He turned to the nurse. "Let's find him some lunch and see if we can't get him out of here by this afternoon."

Mustang sighed. Didn't that figure? The one time he would have actually preferred to remain in the hospital for a while they were sending him home. It looked like his luck hadn't improved much. Though the operation had gone right and his arm would heal. There was no way Mustang could complain about that.

"Grams. I think I'll drive over to the Jackson's. You know, to pick up the plates I brought the empanadas over on and forgot to bring back."

"You don't need to do that, *mija*. Myra said she'd drop them off later in the week. She just couldn't do it today. Michael had his operation today."

As if that hadn't been the only thing on her mind all day. "Yeah, I know. Have you heard from her since?"

Sage's grandmother shook her head. "No, *mija*."

"Oh. I was just wondering how it went. Maybe I should call and see if she needs me to pick anything up for her at the store. I mean, if she's home taking care of Mustang she may not want to leave."

Sage glanced up and saw an amused expression on her grandmother's face. "What?"

"Nothing. I changed my mind. Why don't you go get those plates now, that way you can ask in person if she needs anything. Maybe I'll make more empanadas and try and put some weight on that boy. Make sure you tell him I expect to see him here at least once before he leaves town again."

Before he leaves. That was a very real reminder to Sage. He may be here now, but he would still go away again.

"Okay, Grams. I'll run over right away, you know, to get the plates. I'm just going to get out of my work clothes first."

Her grandmother smiled. "Good idea. Put on that pretty blue dress of yours."

"You don't think it's too much?" She'd worn it to her graduation ceremony and the party afterward.

"No, *mija*. I think it's perfect."

"Okay." Sage nodded and, pulse racing, took off to change clothes.

Chapter Six

"Do you want something else? Ice cream maybe?"

Memories of when he'd had his tonsils out years ago and his mother had given him all the ice cream he wanted had Mustang grinning. "No thanks, Ma. I'm fine."

"I'm just going to get a start on dinner then. You rest."

Apparently she was going to feed him until his arm either healed or he got so fat he couldn't ride bulls anymore.

"Yes, ma'am."

Recuperation on his mama's couch hadn't been as bad as Mustang anticipated so far. Then again, he'd only been released from the hospital for a few hours and his father hadn't gotten home from work yet. He glanced at his watch. He still had another hour or so of peace and quiet. He intended on taking advantage of it.

He'd barely closed his eyes for a little mid-afternoon snooze when there was a light tap on the back door followed by a voice Mustang recognized immediately greeting his mother.

"Can I get you something to drink, darlin'?"

"No, thank you, Mrs. Jackson."

"You let me know if you change your mind. Michael's right inside."

"Thank you, ma'am."

Smiling, he waited for her to come around the corner from the kitchen and when she did, his grin got wider.

"Hey there, Little Bit." Damn she looked good in that blue dress. Mustang's ass was dragging after the surgery, but now she was in the room he felt wide awake.

"How are you feeling?" She kept her voice low, he supposed in deference to his recuperation.

"I'm good." Even better now that she was there.

"You don't have a cast on?" Perched on the edge of the chair next to the couch, she eyed his bandaged arm in the sling.

"Nope. The steel plate or whatever kind of space-age metal they put in me does the job of the cast. I just need the ace bandages and sling for the next few months or so to support it." Hopefully she'd keep visiting regularly and make those months more bearable. "I have to go back in a week and get the staples yanked out of the incision though."

She cringed. Apparently she felt about staples the way he felt about needles. "You know, if you need a ride anywhere while you're here, just give me a call. I'd be happy to drive you wherever you need me to."

He pulled his eyes away from where the neckline of her dress had gaped so he could just see the lacey edge of her bra. "I think I might take you up on that offer."

Sure the doc had said he could drive himself, but having Sage drive him would sure be nice, especially if she was wearing that little number she had on now.

"Okay. Great. I'll give you my cell-phone number." She grabbed the pen from the table where his mother had left it after they'd done the crossword puzzle in the paper together and looked around for something to write on.

Mustang felt in his jeans pocket and came out with a fuel

receipt from when he'd filled up on the highway between Trenton and Magnolia. Had it only been a few days ago that he'd left the circuit and headed home? It felt like a million years, though spending time with his father always felt like that.

He handed the small scrap of paper to her. She jotted down her number and then gave it back to him. Perhaps having that new cell phone wasn't such a bad thing after all. He'd program her number right in, if he could figure out how.

"Thank you, Little Bit."

Her eyes narrowed. "Are you ever going to stop calling me that?"

"Nope." He grinned. If she only knew she had been starring in his painkiller-induced daydreams ever since their meal together.

"Hmm. Maybe I should start calling you Michael again then."

Mustang laughed. "Darlin', you can call me whatever you want."

That offer came out a bit more flirty than it should have considering he'd decided Sage would be off-limits while he was home. Although, what harm could a little innocent flirting do?

One dark eyebrow shot up. "I'll remember that."

"I hope you do." Damn, she could go from innocent to vixen at the drop of a hat. He liked it. Mustang wondered briefly what she'd call him, what terms of endearment she'd use with him in bed. His conscience poked at him. Sage was off-limits.

"I found the video on the Internet from when you broke your arm." Luckily, she changed the subject to safe territory. She touched his good arm lightly. "I'm sorry. I know you're out of competition until the fall."

"How do you know that?" He hadn't even told his parents exactly how long he'd be out of competition, for obvious reasons. If he needed to make an escape from the paternal torture or life as a prison guard, he'd just pretend he was going back to join up with the circuit.

She blushed and lowered her eyes. "I read it on the pro-bull-riders injury report online."

He frowned. "There's an injury report?"

"Yeah. On the Internet." She nodded.

One day he would most likely have to give in and at least learn about computers, if not actually get one. But what was more amazing than his injury being all over the web was Sage. She had actually taken the time to research him online.

Sage was interested and Mustang found that very interesting. She sat so close he could easily admire her dark eyes, inherited from her Mexican grandmother. Then there were those lips, perfectly shaped for kissing. Not to mention those hips he'd love to grab and hold on to tightly while he took them both on a wild ride.

He shook off that thought. "Well, while I'm here, however long that is, it's nice catching up with you again. You and Grams are good people. The kind of people I miss when I'm away."

"And Rosemary too?" She said it and watched him closely, almost like she was waiting for his reaction. "Do you miss her?"

He hadn't exactly been thinking about Rosemary when he was talking about the good people of Magnolia. "Sure. Her too."

Rosemary had always treated Sage like an annoying little sister, when she wasn't outright ignoring her. He supposed he was guilty of ignoring her too a few times near the end. Right before high school graduation when Sage was hanging around them constantly and all he wanted to do was find an opportunity to get his hand in Rosemary's shorts. He'd ended up getting more than his hand in there.

Mustang raised his good arm and brushed a finger down one side of Sage's suddenly somber face. "You sure have grown up. Going to college and working as a teacher. Rosemary has nothing on you."

She finally met his gaze. "There's a thing or two I don't have that she has."

"Are you are talking about a husband and a kid?" He'd learned all about Rosemary marrying Bobby over dinner. Not that Sage had come out and said her sister had trapped her husband into marriage by getting pregnant, but Mustang had read between the lines of Sage's tone and expression. "I wouldn't be so quick to rush into that if I were you. You've got a lot of living to do before all that."

Sage studied him closely for a moment. "You're right. I do have some living to do."

Then she leaned in...

The moment her lips neared his, his body tensed, ready to pounce. When her mouth pressed against his, if he hadn't been in his parents' living room with his mama mere feet away in the next room, he would have had Sage on that couch beneath him before she could say *Woah, Mustang.* Sling be damned.

He wasn't supposed to be kissing Sage. He'd made a deal with himself to steer clear of her while he was home. Maybe if he'd had some clue of what she was about to do, he would have been able to stop it.

Yeah, right. Who was he kidding?

As it was, even with his mother just in the kitchen, Mustang couldn't stop himself from tangling his hand in Sage's hair and holding her mouth tighter against his. He didn't think twice as he tilted his head and plunged his tongue into her mouth. He nearly came in his jeans when she moaned softly against him as her tongue met his.

Then it was over. She pulled away and when he could concentrate again, he heard his father's footsteps on the stairs outside.

His mother appeared in the kitchen doorway. "Do you want to stay and eat with us, Sage? Nothing as good as what you're used to after Maria's cooking, mind you."

With that interruption the moment was gone, but the thrill inside him remained.

"Stay," he whispered, still breathing heavier than normal.

Sage's gaze met his. He saw a need that matched his own there. It seemed like forever before her eyes finally broke away and she answered his mother. "Thank you, Mrs. Jackson. I'd love to."

The front door opened and his father stepped through, his gaze zeroing in on Mustang. "Hmmph. I see you're fine."

Pleasant as ever. "Yes, sir. I am."

"Myra, when's dinner?"

Apparently that was all the concern Mustang was going to get from the man, which was fine with him. Sage was there and that was enough of a distraction to make him forget even about his father.

"In about an hour."

"I'm going to cut the grass quick. Yell when the food's done." His father shot him a look, as if Mustang had been too lazy to cut the grass when he'd gotten home from surgery. Then again, maybe Mustang was just overreacting. He'd had such a chip on his shoulder for most of his life, his father could have brought him a dozen yellow roses in the recovery room and he'd still doubt the man's sincerity.

He sighed and felt Sage's touch on his arm. "My grandmother said to tell you that you better come over and visit her. If you tell me when you feel well enough to go out, I'll come pick you up after I get off work. Any day you want."

Mustang smiled. "How about tomorrow?"

She raised a brow in surprise. "Really? So soon? Will you feel up to it?"

He heard the mower start. An angry sound, though that could have been a reflection of Mustang's own biased opinion. Either way, he didn't want to be around tomorrow evening when his father got home.

Avoiding a confrontation wasn't the only reason Mustang had for wanting to go to the Beckett house the next day. He glanced at Sage, her cheeks still pink and her eyes bright from the intensity of their kiss.

Mustang nodded. "Tomorrow's perfect."

Chapter Seven

It didn't take long for his father to bring up the subject of the job waiting for him at the prison. A whole day.

Actually, that was longer than Mustang figured it would take. He'd assumed the topic would be raised immediately after he got released from the hospital. The most likely reason it hadn't been was Sage's presence. Then tonight Mustang had pulled a disappearing act and gone to her house. It didn't stop his father from hitting him with the question the moment he got home though.

He knew he should have stayed later instead of leaving right after Grams' dessert of fried bananas and ice cream. The food at Sage's house had been as tempting as their one and only kiss. Even if he didn't get the opportunity to repeat it, the heat of the memory was almost enough to make him forget the shitty promise he'd finally made about the job.

Mustang had given in to his father's pressure and agreed to the one thing he thought he'd never do. After he saw the surgeon again next week and got the okay, Mustang would start the daily commute to Huntsville Prison.

His arm felt okay, considering, so of course he'd get the go-ahead to start light work. Wouldn't that be fun? He and his father. Commuting together. Working together. Mustang resisted the strong urge to beat his head against the wall at the idea. Instead, he stared at himself in the mirror above the wooden bureau in his childhood bedroom.

"Three months," he told his reflection. By then he'd either have made enough money working to cover the payments on the trailer until he could get back into competition, or he would have strangled his father on the highway somewhere between Magnolia and Huntsville.

Either way, he was out of here after twelve weeks. Shit. Calculating his time in weeks still sounded worse than it did in months no matter how often he tried it out.

It didn't matter. He could do it, he *would* do it. A man could withstand anything for a limited amount of time. He proved that every time he rode a ton of bucking bovine to the buzzer.

Thoughts of riding again caused Mustang to sigh. Missing life on the road with the pro circuit, he eyed his cell phone on the dresser. He supposed he could call Slade, though that would only make him miss it more.

Calling Sage now was probably out of the question too. They'd just seen each other less than an hour before.

How pitiful was he? Debating on whether to call a girl. Usually he was in and out, literally, but Sage was different. She was a friend as well as a girl who made him stand up and take notice. As his head warred with his dick, he wasn't sure if that was good or bad. Could a woman be both to a man?

His brain was too tired to think anymore tonight, even though it was still early. Time to get undressed and hit the hay. What else could he do? Sit on the couch between his mother and father and watch television like when he was a kid? He definitely should have stayed later at Sage's.

Too late now.

Pulling his wallet out of his jeans pocket, Mustang tossed it on top of the bureau. It skidded across the wood, coming to rest against the base of the lamp as a white card slipped out of the fold. He frowned. Whose business card would he have in his wallet?

Mustang read the name and smiled. Guy the sports photographer. He'd forgotten all about him. What had Chase said that job paid? A couple of hundred an hour or something like that. Hell, that was way better than what he'd get being tortured by his father at the prison. But shit, this guy was in New Jersey.

He knew he should have stayed on the East Coast. Maybe Mustang could contact him and set up some shoots in a week or two. If the guy promised him a guaranteed income, maybe he wouldn't have to work with his father at all. He could recuperate for a few weeks then drive back to Jersey.

Mustang grabbed his phone, vowing never to admit to either Slade or Jenna how dependant he'd become on it.

It was pretty late in New Jersey for a business to be open, but he could leave a message. The photographer could call him back in the morning. He punched in the numbers and listened to the ring. Mustang jumped when a live voice rather than a machine greeted him.

"Guy Little."

He stumbled over his tongue at having to talk to a person when he was expecting to leave a voicemail. "Hey, um, yeah. I have your card here. About the sports modeling."

Modeling. Who would have thought he'd ever willingly do that? But hell, he was a decent-looking man, even with the assorted scars. Why not make some money off it? Desperate times called for desperate measures.

"Great. Tell me a little about yourself."

"Um. Okay. I'm a bull rider. Um, just about six feet tall. A hundred seventy pounds, give or take. Light brown hair. Blue eyes."

"How old are you."

"Twenty-six." Was that too old for a sports model? Mustang didn't know. In fact, he knew shit about this whole deal.

"Okay. Good. Tell me, do you have a problem with nudity?"

Mustang stopped dead mid-pace across his room. "Mine, or someone else's?"

Maybe they were going to have some scantily clad female in a thong hanging on him while he was dressed in his gear. That would be cool.

The man laughed. "Yours, but I like how you think."

"What? Wait, I'd be naked?"

"Partially. We do artistic nudes."

Whatever the hell that meant.

He'd said partially. They probably just wanted some pictures with his shirt off. That was fine. His muscles weren't huge but he was fit. He'd have to figure out how to hide the incision from the operation though.

"That's all right, I guess."

"I'd want some with you dressed in your bull-riding stuff too. Do you own a pair chaps?"

"Sure." More than one actually, thanks to the new pair he'd won in a bet against Slade last year.

"And boots and a cowboy hat?"

"Yeah." What self-respecting Texan didn't own boots and a hat? Then again, this guy was in New Jersey so Mustang gave him a pass.

"Great. Bring that all with you when you come in."

"Well, you see, that's the problem. I'm not in New Jersey anymore—" Mustang rushed to add, "—but I can get back there if you just give me some time."

"Where are you now?"

"Texas?"

"That's fine. I've got a photographer who works with me out there. Can you get to Houston?"

"Hell, yeah. No problem."

He heard the sound of papers rustling. "Perfect, I'll have him call you. His name is Joe. Let me get your name and number."

"It's Mustang Jackson."

The man laughed. "Mustang, huh? Perfect. I love it. Should he call you at this number or a different one?"

Mustang's spirits soared. This could work. This crazy scheme could save his sanity and prevent him from having to work with his father. "This number is good. Uh, can I ask you what the pay is?"

"One hundred and fifty an hour, flat fee and you'll have to sign a full release. You have a problem with that?"

"No, that's fine." He had to sign releases all the time saying he wouldn't sue the arena if he got hurt riding. That was pretty standard. Though how he'd get hurt modeling he didn't know.

"Okay, we're set then."

Yes, they were and he couldn't be happier. After saying goodbye and disconnecting with Guy, Mustang glanced down at the phone in his hand and couldn't resist sharing his happiness. He found Sage's cell-phone number easily in his very short contact list and called, waiting for her sweet, "Hello?"

Mustang grinned just from the sound of her voice. "Hey, Little Bit."

"Mustang. Hi." He could hear her smile.

"Guess what?"

"What?"

"I got a job modeling." He would rather die than admit what he was doing to any of the guys or to his parents, but for some reason telling Sage felt right.

"Modeling?" Her voice rose to a squeak.

He laughed, really laughed. Deep from his belly. "Yup and don't sound so shocked. I'm a good-looking guy. Aren't I?"

"Yes, and so modest too." She laughed.

"Actually, the photographer's never seen me so I may be sent packing before he even takes one picture. Besides, it's for a sports website, not GQ Magazine or anything fancy like that." Mustang stretched out on his bed, relaxing. It felt good to have the pressure of the sling no longer weighing around his neck.

"I don't know. You could be in GQ if you wanted, I think. I saw you dressed up for the prom." Sage's voice softened.

Mustang held the phone closer to his ear so he could enjoy every nuance of every sound. "Yeah, I guess I do clean up pretty good."

"Mmm, hmm. You do. I remember you in your tuxedo with your black cowboy boots."

He laughed again. "Those new boots cost me a fortune and all your sister did was complain I wasn't wearing real shoes. She wanted me to get those stupid lace-up black things they had at the tux rental place."

"I liked your boots. You looked perfect."

Mustang's breath caught in his throat at the sincerity with which she'd delivered that incredibly touching compliment. "Thanks."

"You're welcome."

"I should let you go. You probably have stuff to do that I'm keeping you from." Though the last thing he wanted to do was hang up with her.

"No, not really."

He heard the lie in her voice. She'd always been the worst liar. "No homework? You sure?"

"Well, maybe a little."

"I thought so." Still, he didn't say the words good bye.

"Mustang?"

"Yeah?" His voice sounded husky in his own ears and he cleared his throat.

"I really liked our kiss the other night."

His pulse sped. "Me too."

One more statement like that out of her and he'd be over there and sneaking into her bedroom window in a heart beat.

"Do you want to come over again for dinner sometime this week? Maybe tomorrow or the next night?"

"Yes." Tomorrow and the next night and every night after that...until he left. The thought of leaving and not being able to see Sage twisted his gut. He swallowed hard.

He was in deep shit.

Chapter Eight

"Great. Can you open your shirt?" Joe spoke without lowering the camera, but Mustang was getting used to that after the dozens of shots the guy had already taken.

"Sure." Mustang used his right hand to unbutton the shirt, pretending that his left arm was just fine.

He'd taken off the bandages, covered the incision in clear surgical tape and not worn the sling to the photo shoot hoping the photographer wouldn't notice.

Even if they made him take his shirt totally off and decided they couldn't use him because of the scar, they were too far into it already. He'd still get an hour's pay. Well worth the drive to Houston.

Striking a few poses, he was still feeling a little awkward. He was used to being photographed, but at sporting events. There they took action shots. None of this posing and "turn slightly to the left and stare at the floor to your right" crap.

"Perfect." Joe lowered the camera and fiddled with something on it. "Let's try a few without the jeans."

Mustang whipped his head around. "Excuse me?"

"Just the chaps, no jeans."

"You mean you want me in my underwear with my chaps?" Which underwear was he wearing, anyway? He hoped not the ripped pair. And why the hell did the guy want a picture of that? That wasn't attractive.

Joe laughed. "No, Mustang. No underwear. Just the chaps."

"You mean...with my business hanging out?" He frowned.

The photographer smirked. "Your *business*. I haven't heard it called that before but yeah, that's what we want."

People on a sports website wanted to see that? "Where are these pictures going again?"

"The site's not up yet. Didn't Guy give you the web address?"

"Yeah. It's on his business card."

"He told you there'd be nudity, right?"

"Yeah." Guy had said artistic nudity. What the hell was artistic about his dick? Joe waited expectantly until Mustang continued. "I'm just not sure why anyone would want to see me naked, is all."

Especially on a site dedicated to sports.

"You'd be surprised. Believe me." Joe shook his head.

Mustang really needed to get a computer and learn how to use it, especially if his cock was going to be out there in public on it.

"How many more hours do you think we'll be shooting?"

"At least another hour."

Three hundred dollars minimum. Just for some pictures. He couldn't pass that up. Mustang sighed and started to unbuckle his pants. Then he had a thought and pulled his hat down lower over his eyes. "You think maybe we can put a fake name up there on the website though? So no one knows it's me?"

"You mean Mustang is your real name?" The shock showed

clearly on Joe's face.

"Yeah, well, I mean it's the name I ride under and everyone knows me by that name. So maybe I shouldn't be doing this under the same name."

"Don't worry about it. They'll make up something good for you."

"Okay." Feeling better about that at least, Mustang started to unbuckle his chap straps, all while Joe looked on. That was creepy enough, but not half as bad as when he pushed his jeans and then underwear down to his ankles.

Mustang suddenly had the urge to cover himself with both hands and run naked for the hills.

He buckled his chaps back on as quickly as he could, happy for any sort of coverage, even though the damn things didn't cover any of the important stuff. Not in the back or the front.

"Take the shirt totally off too. It's covering you up."

Shit. Unhappily, Mustang did as he was told. He didn't give a damn anymore whether the photographer saw his incision or not. Right now he was more worried about the fact that the man was zooming that big, long lens in on his dick.

When he thought things couldn't get any worse, Joe said, "That's great. For these next round of shots, can you get yourself hard? There's some baby oil over on the table, if you need it."

Holy crap. What the hell had he gotten himself into?

Mustang drove home with three hundred dollars cash in his pocket and shaking hands. He could barely concentrate on keeping the trailer on the road as he argued with himself. So he had been pretty much naked in a room with a strange man. Big deal. The guy hadn't touched him or anything. Men were naked together in locker rooms all the time.

Though it was frigging creepy to have Joe studying him through the lens of that camera and—God help him—directing him about what to do with himself.

Shit. He felt...violated. He considered if he'd feel differently if the photographer had been a female. If a hot woman with a camera had been focused on him, telling him to rub his cock and get it hard for her, yeah, that would have been hugely different.

He sighed. Three hundred was just a drop in the bucket of what he needed to cover his expenses over the next few months. His dreams for a big, high-paying modeling career were shot after today. If this was what modeling was like, they could keep it. A hundred and fifty an hour wasn't worth it.

Now he'd have to work with his father *and* live with the memories of standing in nothing but chaps while he stroked himself into semi-erectness in front of a man. It was no wonder he hadn't been able to get totally hard. He wasn't into men. Add to that the air conditioner cranking on high so the room was frigid. Who the hell could have gotten it up in those conditions? It was a miracle he'd been able to get even partially hard.

Great, naked and almost impotent for all the world to see, all for a measly three hundred dollars. The fine imposed on a rider for challenging the judges' decision in competition was more than that.

A chill ran down his spine at the memory of it all. He needed a drink, or even better, to sink himself into a nice, soft woman. Sage crossed his mind and he quickly dismissed the idea.

Mustang passed the turnoff to Sage's house and glanced at it wistfully. Hell, Sage was a good friend and he really needed to talk. He tapped the brake with his foot and considered swinging the trailer into a U-turn.

She would be sitting down at the small old table in the corner of the kitchen. The one they used when they didn't have company. She probably had her legs curled up and her feet tucked under her like a little kid. That had been her favorite position to eat in when they were younger. When he'd eaten over this week he noticed she still did it.

What would Grams have put on the table for dinner? Something light since it was hot today. *Pico de gallo* maybe, made with cool cucumber and melon and drenched in tangy fresh citrus juice and spicy hot pepper.

His mouth started to water and he yanked his mind away from the thought of Gram's cooking and hit the gas. He couldn't think about food without his stomach protesting since he'd skipped eating before he'd left for the shoot. He didn't want to think about the shoot either.

His mind traveled back to Sage, the one subject that he thought would be safe, until the fantasy of her there at the photo shoot helping him get hard sprung into his mind.

Damn. He definitely couldn't go knocking on her door now. He needed to get home and take a shower. Wash away that oil Joe had him spread all over himself for those pictures and the memories that went along with it.

Mustang took the next turn onto his parents' street as his cell phone rang. He knew instinctively who it was before a glance at the caller ID told him.

"Hey, Little Bit."

"How did the shoot go?"

He sighed. She was the only one on earth who knew about

the photo shoot, except for the photographer. He could tell her it went fine and never talk about it again. Hell, he could tell her he didn't go at all, that the guy canceled, and that would be it too. But if Mustang was going to purge this awful, uncomfortable feeling by talking about it with anyone at all, it would be to her.

"Well, not so good."

"Oh no. What happened?"

When the hell had his life gotten so fucked up? He glanced down at the sling on the seat next to him, the one he'd have to slip on before his mother noticed he'd taken it off. Yup, about the time he'd gotten that sling was when his life had taken a nosedive for the pavement, but he wouldn't need it forever. If one thing was true it was that Mustang Jackson would land on his feet. Eventually.

Sage would tell him it was okay. That artistic nudes were perfectly all right. Then he'd feel better. He swallowed hard and launched into his account.

"Well, it started out kind of weird because I'm not used to that kind of stuff, but then things got weirder..."

Chapter Nine

Day one as a prison guard working with his old man had been about as bad as he'd expected it to be. His father's consistent introduction to everyone they met during his grand tour of the facility was an added bonus Mustang hadn't anticipated.

"This here's my fool son, Michael. He broke his arm riding a bull, but now he's ready to tackle a real man's job."

In spite of that less-than-illustrious beginning to his temporary prison guard career, Mustang went back for more punishment. Day two of working at Huntsville Prison with his father didn't go any better than day one had. In fact, it was infinitely worse.

Mustang got caught asleep in front of the video monitors. In his defense, the task was the most boring on earth. Even all the coffee he'd drunk didn't help keep him stimulated while sitting in the tiny, windowless room staring at a bunch of screens. Mustang could practically feel his muscles atrophying from the inactivity, but his father insisted he couldn't perform any other duty at the prison with one arm in a sling.

The drive home had been filled with his father's angry lecture about how Mustang had embarrassed him, followed by the inevitable, "It's hard for me to believe you're actually my son." Then he'd added the real clincher, "Thank God your grandfather is dead and didn't see your performance today."

Thank God your grandfather's dead. Yeah. Real nice.

Then there was the angry silent treatment for the remainder of the drive, which Mustang preferred actually.

His mother didn't need more than one glance at their faces when they walked through the front door to determine their moods. She didn't ask how work had been. Instead she announced, "Dinner in half an hour."

"Thanks, Ma. I'm going to shower."

She nodded and disappeared into the kitchen, probably as anxious to escape his father's recount of the day as Mustang was.

The stiff fabric of Mustang's blue polyester uniform pants swished as he dragged himself into the bedroom. He hadn't even worked a full week yet. What else was he in for?

He pulled his wallet and phone out of the pocket and flung them onto the dresser. He crossed the small room and flopped back on the bed after the day from hell.

Not even one week down and three more months to go. Perhaps he should break it down into days and tick them off with marks on his wall next to the bed like the prisoners did. That seemed apt.

He needed a drink. He needed a nap. He needed a woman. Most of all, he needed to get the hell away from his father.

The cell phone rang. Three whole people had that number. Slade, whom he'd just talked to yesterday, Jenna and Sage. Oh wait. There were a few more now. Guy and Joe, the questionable photographers. Hmm, he'd only had the damn phone a little over a week and he was already filling up his address book.

Hauling himself off the bed, he grabbed the cell and

glanced at the number.

He flipped it open with a smile. "Sage."

"Hey. I wanted to see how your first week of work is going."

He groaned. "Is your grandmother within hearing distance?"

"No. I'm in my bedroom alone."

Mustang enjoyed a quick fantasy of Sage lying on her belly on the bed wearing nothing but a T-shirt and a little pair of cheek-bearing undies, feet kicked up in the air as she talked.

"Good. If she can't hear then I can safely tell you my job fucking sucks." His entire life sucked at the moment.

"Oh, no. I'm so sorry. What happened?"

"Well, let's see. It started when my father presented me with my very own uniform and it all went downhill from there." He flopped back onto his own bed, holding the phone to his ear. He stared up at the ceiling and realized the last thing he wanted to do was recount his day. "Can we change the subject? I'm starting to get depressed. What did you do today?"

"Hmm. I wiped some snotty noses, cleaned up a massive glue spillage and oh, yeah, did a dramatic reading of *Thomas the Train*."

Mustang laughed. "You have a position opening up there anytime soon? That sounds much better than my day."

She laughed. "I'll see what I can do, but in the meantime, how would you feel about a picnic down by the lake?"

"Tonight?"

"Yup. It's beautiful out."

He hadn't noticed, having been ensconced in hell and all. "Sure. Just let me shower and change and I'll meet you there."

"Sounds good. See you there."

Mustang told his mother he was going out and luckily, once she heard it was with Sage, she didn't seem to mind he was skipping out on dinner. Then he showered, plastic bag covering his bandages and all. He'd be very happy when this arm was healed for so many reasons.

Finally, changed into normal clothes and feeling better, he headed out on foot for the lake that lay halfway between his and Sage's house. It was probably a mile to drive to her house, but by taking the shortcut and cutting through backyards the way he used to when he was a kid, he was there in just a few minutes.

He arrived to find her already there. She was bent over a basket. He yanked his eyes off her ass as she stood, a folded blanket held in her hand.

"Hey there." He grinned with the sheer joy of seeing her.

"You look like you're in a better mood."

He took the blanket from her and she helped him spread it out on the grass. "Yes, I am."

Sage swung the picnic basket onto the corner of the blanket and sat on her knees facing him. "Oh, really? And why is that?"

Mustang sat too, stretching his legs out in front of him. "Because I know you and Grams packed something good in that basket."

If only she knew the truth about why he was smiling. He tried to get comfortable without leaning on his bad arm. He finally ended up rolling on one side and propping his head up with his right hand. From that position, he was about eyelevel with Sage's absolutely beautiful breasts.

More and more women were getting big, fake implants. Not Sage though. Her breasts were perfect. He imagined taking a nipple into his mouth then shook that image from his brain.

"So work sucked, huh? I'm sorry."

"Yup." Mustang shrugged. "It will be a relief when I don't have to depend on that man and owe him for that stupid job I never wanted anyway."

"I guess you could always become a full-time model and quit the prison." She grinned devilishly.

He rolled his eyes. "No, thanks. I don't want to talk about the prison or that stupid modeling job. Tell me more about what you did today."

She groaned and crossed her legs, tucking her dress down between them. "Hmm, let's see. After school I came home and did my own schoolwork for my college classes."

He smiled at the tiny wrinkle that had appeared between her brows when she talked about homework. "Oh, that sounds like a ton of fun. You wild woman."

"I had to get it done if I wanted to do something fun with you tonight. See? I had a plan."

Yes, she did and so did he. His plan was to get out of this town as soon as possible. Unfortunately, other parts of him had mutinied and were currently plotting on how to get his hands and mouth on Sage as soon as possible.

Sage was sweet and innocent and tempting as hell, and she didn't fit into his plans. One night with Sage might make him want to stick around. He didn't want to want that. He wanted to go join up with Slade. The only reason stopping him from rejoicing at the thought of doing exactly that was seated in front of him looking entirely too tempting.

She was watching him with those eyes of hers that a man could get lost in and something suddenly struck him.

"Where did your glasses go?"

Sage smiled. "I got contacts my freshman year in high

school."

He'd already left town by then. Whenever it had happened, he was glad it had. "I'd always thought it was a shame to hide such pretty eyes behind glasses."

"You did not." She scowled. "You never looked close enough to see my eyes back then."

Mustang frowned. "That's not true. I swear. I always thought you were a pretty girl, even when you had on those ugly braces with the pink and green rubber bands."

She laughed. "Thanks, I guess. And those were the hottest fashion colors in braces back then, I'll have you know."

He considered carefully how he'd remembered those details from over a decade ago. If his life depended on it, he couldn't tell you the eye color of the last woman he'd been with, even though he'd spent a good portion of that night having sex with her. He'd even faced her during some of it. Yet he remembered so many details about Sage and he probably would even after he left Magnolia again.

He pressed one hand to the sinking feeling in his belly at the thought of leaving. He noticed her watching him and scrambled for something to say. "Maybe we can eat now."

"Sure, we can do that. Are you feeling all right? Are you still on pills from the operation? I know they can mess with your stomach."

"I'm finally done with the antibiotics and I'm basically off the painkillers too. I took one last night when I got achy and couldn't sleep but today I didn't take any."

Luckily the discussion about medicine gave him something to think about besides wanting her and knowing he shouldn't have her, but even that didn't prevent him from focusing one hundred percent on the shape of her ass as she turned away from him and bent to open the basket of food.

He pictured nestling up closely behind her. Sliding his hands onto each of her hips. Holding her close. She turned and he realized she was watching him and waiting expectantly.

"Um, sorry. What did you say?"

She smiled. "You really must have had a tough day at work. You seem a million miles away. I asked if you wanted something to drink."

God, yes. Bourbon, straight up. "What have you got?"

"Water or sweet tea."

He laughed. What else would a sweet innocent girl have to offer by way of drinks? "Sweet tea is good. Thanks."

She handed it to him. He had to sit up to be able to grab it.

"My grandmother made your favorite."

"Empanadas?"

Sage nodded. "Yup. I'll have you know I have to beg her to make them for me. Now that she's just cooking for the two of us, I usually only get them on my birthday and a few other times during the year. But you come home and she's made them twice already."

He shrugged, smiling. "What can I say? I have a way with the ladies. I'm just a charmer, I guess."

"Yes, you are." The expression on her face became serious. She leaned in closer, taking his sweet tea out of his hand and putting it down on the ground. Then her mouth was too close to resist, so he didn't.

Whether she or he closed the final distance he didn't know or care, but it seemed they were drawn together like two magnets.

As soon as their lips touched he sank into absolute bliss. Somehow he ended up on his back with her on top of him. Her leg lodged between his so her hip pressed against the zipper in his jeans. He didn't dare move or risk losing the contact that felt so good.

Her tongue slipped into his mouth. He tilted his head to take more of her inside him. Wrapping his arm around her, he pressed her to him, not willing to let her get away.

Mustang felt her grind her crotch against his thigh. Her breathing quickened as she rubbed against him. He groaned, so turned on he couldn't stand it.

Kissing him like her life depended on it, she started to tremble in his arms. He broke the kiss and pulled back to watch her face. Eyes squeezed shut, mouth open, she was enough to make a man lose all control. It took every shred of control he had to not flip her over, raise that skirt and fuck her silly. He'd never seen a woman look so beautifully tempting.

"Oh God, Sage." He drew in a shaky breath.

That brought her out of it and she tried to roll off of him, but he held tight. Turning pink in the cheeks, she finally met his gaze. "I'm sorry."

"Are you crazy. That was the hottest thing I've ever experienced. *Don't* be sorry." He grabbed her head with his right hand and kissed the embarrassment from her face.

Cursing his sling, he had to satisfy himself with holding her with one arm while she lay above him. He was hard as a rock, there was no way she could miss feeling him pressing against her, but he didn't move. Neither did she as she stared down at him with those deep chocolate eyes. "Do you still want to eat?"

Mustang laughed and shook his head at the X-rated image that flitted through his head. She had no idea what he was picturing eating. Good thing she meant food.

"Yeah, sure. Let's eat."

They had better do something to distract him because the

impulse to make love to her was nearly overwhelming. In spite of what he wanted, he let her roll off him.

What was he going to do for the next few months if they couldn't even eat together without his wanting to plunge inside her?

She delivered a paper plate laden with food and handed it to him. "Your favorite kind."

"Onion and jalapeno?"

"Of course."

"For both of us? Your favorite is chicken."

She blushed. "You remembered that?"

"Of course."

Still pink cheeked, she laughed. "Wow. Well anyway, yeah, for both of us. Grams only made your favorite kind."

"Because I'm so charming, remember?"

From the way she dropped her eyes, she was remembering. He smiled, happy they'd both taste like onions just in case there was a repeat of that kiss. His pulse raced at the thought.

Getting excited over just kissing. He was reliving his high school years all over again. Funny how he didn't mind it one bit.

An hour or so later, back at his house with memories of a damn nice goodbye kiss from Sage to keep him warm, Mustang walked into his bedroom.

Emptying his pockets so he could ditch his jeans and go rub out the need being near Sage all evening had created, Mustang pulled out his cell phone just as it began to ring. Glancing at the readout, he didn't recognize the number but that didn't mean much.

It was a Houston area code. Maybe Joe wanted him to pose mostly naked for his sports site again. Perhaps this time he'd be in football gear since he had mentioned he'd played a bit in high school. Another week of work like this past one and he might jump at that chance.

"Hello."

A female voice greeted him. "Mustang Jackson?"

Uh oh. Who was this and what did she want? Reviewing the dozens of women he'd spent one night with while he'd crisscrossed this country as well as Canada and Mexico for competitions, Mustang suddenly remembered why he'd never gotten a cell phone before. But how the hell could any one of them have gotten this number? "Um, who's calling?"

"My name is Missy Love. I run a video production company and I was contacted by Joe Parisi about a cowboy named Mustang Jackson who has what I need for a video we're shooting this weekend."

Mustang's eyebrows shot up. "Really. And what kind of video would this be?"

"Are you Mustang?"

What the hell, he might as well admit to it. "Yeah, I'm Mustang."

"Great. It's nice to talk to you. Joe spoke very highly about your photo session."

"He did? Huh. Okay. So what kind of video is this? If you're looking to film me in action, I have to be honest. I've just had surgery on my arm and I can't ride right now."

She laughed. "I'm looking for action, but not that kind. Mustang, I produce adult videos."

Holy crap! "You mean porn?"

"We don't like to use that term in this industry. It gives the wrong impression. What we produce are high-quality adult videos for use as sexual aids by couples in a committed relationship."

Yeah, and he read titty magazines for the articles. Whatever you called it, he couldn't believe she wanted him.

"I've never done anything like that before." He wasn't so sure he wanted to.

"It's fine if you don't have prior experience. We'd want you to come in a little early before filming starts for kind of an orientation. We'll show you around set and introduce you to the cast and crew. Oh, and you'll have to go for testing."

"Go for what?" Mustang stifled a laugh. Orientation and testing? This was sounding more like getting into college than porn.

"All our performers are tested regularly for both HIV and STDs. You'd have to agree to that before I can contract you. You can go to your regular doctor if you'd like. Or any one of the health clinics in the area will do the testing too."

Wow. Mustang sat down on the edge of his bed before he fell down. This woman really wanted him to fuck on camera. For money. "Yeah. Testing is fine. Um, how much cash are we talking about here?"

"Oh, we don't pay in cash. We'd pay you by check on the books. Our performers are paid as independent contractors and are all required to fill out the appropriate forms and file income taxes on their earnings. However, if your question was what we pay, that's fifteen hundred a movie."

Fifteen hundred. His mind reeled figuring out how long he'd have to work in prison hell to earn that much. "How long does a movie take to shoot?"

"We'll get it done in one day. I have the location booked for

Saturday. Are you available?"

Mustang's heart kicked into high gear. Fifteen hundred dollars for one day. "You really don't care that I don't have experience in this stuff? I mean, don't get me wrong, I've been with plenty of women, I just mean the video part."

"That's what we like about you. We're looking for a new face and Joe said you had the assets we look for."

"Assets?"

What were those? Blue eyes? No beer gut? He didn't want to even consider Joe's reporting on his most obvious *asset*.

"Not to be indelicate, but Joe's exact words were that you're 'hung like a horse'."

Mustang swallowed hard, fighting the disturbing feeling crawling up his spine that the male photographer had said that about him, true or not.

"I'm sorry. Did I offend you, Mr. Jackson?"

Her question knocked him out of his silence. "No. It's okay. And call me Mustang. Um. Wait, that's another thing. Can I use a different name?"

"Of course. That's standard in the business to protect the actors."

What Slade had said last year when he thought Jenna was a reporter looking to write an exposé about them and their sexual exploits flitted through Mustang's brain. Basically something about how the fans in the Bible Belt would never accept a rider who had a bad reputation with women.

He needed to protect more than his name. Mustang needed to protect his career too. What if a fan recognized his face or the press got a hold of the video?

"Any chance we can film me with my cowboy hat on so my face doesn't show too much?"

"You're in luck. We're filming on a ranch so yeah, I think that will work fine for the script."

"A script? Do I have a lot of lines to memorize?"

She laughed. "No. Not too many at all. Don't worry. So are we good? If everything tests well at the doctor, you'll take the job?"

He swallowed a lump from his throat. How could he say no? "Yeah, I'll take it."

"I have more shoots scheduled I could use you for if things work out Saturday. We'll see how you do. Okay?"

"Okay." One movie and he'd have a nice chunk of money for payments on the trailer. Two movies and he could probably quit his job at the prison and still be okay with expenses for three or four months.

"Great. Let me give you the information."

Ignoring his gut reaction to the sex-with-a-stranger-on-camera-for-money concept, he glanced around his bedroom. "Okay. Hang on. Let me find a pen and paper."

He was really going to do this. Fuck for money. Holy crap. Mustang put the phone down and ran a hand over his face, trying to rub away the absurdity of the idea. He wasn't sure if he should feel like the luckiest man in the world or like some pitiful male hooker. Either way, making that kind of money for one day's work was a dream come true. If this thing panned out, this could be the last week he'd have to be dependent and under his father's thumb.

Chapter Ten

"Hey, Mustang."

Driving down the road early Saturday morning while trying to follow the directions to the ranch for his first porno-movie shoot, Mustang hadn't bothered to check the caller ID before he answered the cell phone. Now he wished he had. Sage's voice, full of sweet, innocent exuberance made him feel like the devil on earth.

"Sage. Um, hey."

"I was wondering if you wanted to get together. You're off from work today, right? I thought you might want to do something fun."

He smothered a bitter laugh. Normally, he'd think of a full day of fucking as fun, but somehow he wasn't exactly looking forward it today.

Remembering the kind of "fun" he and Sage had at the lake brought on a whole other wave of guilt. They were by no means dating, and all they'd done was kiss, but it felt like he was about to cheat on her.

Worse than that, he'd gotten used to telling her about everything. Even the embarrassing stuff like the nude-modeling thing. But this he couldn't tell her about. He was afraid if she knew she'd never want to talk to him again.

But he needed the money. Maybe she'd understand that. Though maybe not. He had a job. A good job according to his father anyway. He didn't have to do this.

He decided to keep his mouth shut. He couldn't risk losing her friendship. Besides, maybe it wouldn't work out. Maybe this woman wouldn't even want him in the movie. Then he could drive home, find Sage and pretend nothing had ever happened.

"Um, I can't. Sorry. I have, uh, plans." He had to get off the phone with her before he changed his mind about doing this.

"Oh. Okay." She became strangely silent.

"It's, you know, work related." That wasn't exactly a lie and she had sounded so disappointed, he had to explain somehow. "Maybe tomorrow? I could do something then."

Sage perked up a bit. "Sure. Call me. Okay?"

"I will, Little Bit. Thanks for thinking of me. Bye for now."

"Bye for now." He heard the smile in her voice.

Shit. He tossed the phone onto the passenger seat and slammed on the brakes, taking a sharp right as he almost missed the turn to the ranch.

There it was in front of him. The entrance gate. Two workmen balanced a sign as a third man on a ladder screwed it into place above the drive. Mustang slowed the trailer and read, "Double P Ranch".

Oh, God. The plot of this movie, what there would be of it, was beginning to form. He should have asked for more details before he agreed to this thing.

One man waved him through the gate and he drove at a crawl up the driveway, not anxious to arrive anytime soon. The house sprawled before him, but most of the action seemed to be centered around the barn. He pulled over next to a van and parked.

People bustled about and for the first time he really began to comprehend that every last one of them would be there to watch him having sex with a strange woman.

God, he hoped it was a woman. He hadn't asked. What if it was gay porn? Shit! If it was, he'd leave. That's all. No harm, no foul.

A short blonde carrying a clipboard and wearing a business suit and an earpiece came rushing toward him. "Mustang?"

"Yeah."

She smiled. "Missy Love."

He shook the hand she extended but wasn't sure what to say, so he didn't say anything at all. She didn't seem to notice as she turned and began running down a list of instructions for him. He scrambled to follow. She may have short legs but she moved fast.

"Your HIV and STD test results came back fine so we're good there." Missy glanced sideways at him. "I was prepared with clothes for the shoot, but what you have on looks good. We'll keep you in that."

Keeping him in clothes sounded good to him.

"Your co-stars are already here so let's find them and introduce you."

Them, as in more than one. He swallowed. "Who will I be, um, working with?"

"Arizona. You may have heard of her, she won the adult film star award last year for best female lead, and Jon Long. He's been in the industry forever. You'll recognize him."

He didn't dare tell her that he'd seen a grand total of two porno movies in his life and didn't really follow the adult film awards. "I, uh, saw the sign they were putting up over the gate."

She grinned at him. "Yeah. Isn't that great? That's the

name of the film too. *The Double P*. Clever, huh?"

"Yeah. So I guess that we'll be..."

He never got to finish his question since she was already talking to someone through the thing attached to her ear. Then she was shouting to someone else about lighting. In the midst of it all he was thrust at an unhappy-looking woman and two men.

"Hey, guys. This is Mustang. Introduce yourselves. He's a newbie so give him the rundown for me, okay? I've got to handle some stuff. We start shooting in fifteen."

Fifteen minutes. He guessed this "rundown" was his orientation. It wasn't what he'd pictured, but then again, he'd had no frigging clue what to expect.

A man wearing a robe and he suspected nothing else shook his hand. "I'm Jon Long. Mustang, huh? Great stage name."

"Actually, Mustang isn't a stage name. I guess I need to come up with one though." He'd forgotten about that part.

"Too bad. Mustang gives the fans certain expectations, you know?" Jon Long, whose name also provided a certain level of expectation, winked at him. The bushy, black sideburns gave the man an unsavory appearance. That made Mustang even more uncomfortable that in less than fifteen minutes, he'd be getting naked, up close and personal with him. He really hoped it wouldn't be too close or too personal.

The hair on the back of his neck stood up at that thought so he turned to the only woman among them. "Hi. I um, guess we'll be uh, working together."

The woman, who must be Arizona since she was clad in a robe too, blew out a breath while shaking her head. "Another newbie."

He stifled the urge to apologize to her for his lack of adult-film experience all while wondering how in the world he was going to be able to "perform". One diva bitch, an aging seventies throwback and a live audience made up of the crew did not make for the ideal conditions for Junior to want to come out and play.

"Hey. I'm Clint. Arizona's boyfriend." The man standing next to Arizona stepped forward and introduced himself, and the situation—unbelievably—got even worse.

Her *what?*

"Hey. I'm Mustang Jackson." Mustang shook the hand of the boyfriend of the girl he was about to fuck.

"*The* Mustang Jackson? The bull rider? Former Rookie of the Year?"

Crap. Clint knew about him. "Uh, yeah."

"Oh, man. I can't believe it's really you. I saw your last ride in Trenton on television. What the fuck happened there? One minute you were scoring ninety and the next they were saying you were on your way to the hospital."

How strange was this conversation?

"Yeah. I broke my ulna." He'd left the sling in the truck, but he held up his left arm anyway. "I guess I should mention that to Missy. The doc put in a plate and some screws so I can use it a bit but I can't, you know, support my full body weight with it yet."

"Great." Arizona rolled her eyes. "I'm going to fix my makeup."

"No problem, Mustang. Don't worry. We'll work around your arm." Jon ignored Arizona's exit as if he was used to it.

Mustang watched their female co-star walking away in a huff. "Did I say something wrong? Usually it takes more than a minute for me to piss a woman off."

Clint shook his head. "It's not you, man. She's just sick of working with newbies. Missy has been on this kick lately to discover new talent, but Arizona is the one that has to deal with their bullshit."

"Maybe I shouldn't do this. I really don't know what I'm doing."

"You'll be fine. Just follow my lead." Jon adjusted the belt on his robe, tying it tighter. Mustang was happy for that. He didn't need a preview right now.

"Yeah. Jon's a veteran. And I can give you some pointers so you don't piss off Arizona, if you want," Clint offered.

Mustang noticed his hands were starting to tremble the closer they came to doing this. He shoved them in his pockets. "I'd appreciate that."

"First of all, no getting handy with her." Clint began to tick off his tips for not pissing off porn stars. Maybe the man should write a *Porn for Dummies* book.

"What do you mean *handy*? I can't touch her? But then how can I...you know."

"You can touch her, just don't act like a boyfriend. That really gets her going."

Mustang frowned. They were going to be having sex for God's sake. That's what boyfriends and girlfriends did. "I'm not sure what you mean."

"Don't act too familiar. You know?"

This was the most surreal conversation Mustang had ever experienced. Talking with a man who was giving him pointers on how best to fuck his girlfriend. How the hell could a man watch the woman he loved doing other men? He'd go crazy.

Mustang stopped dead at that thought. He remembered how Slade had freaked out when the two of then were both with

Jenna. Maybe he did understand how Slade felt. Mustang just hadn't wanted to see his side back then because he was enjoying the sex too much.

His attention back on Clint, Mustang was still confused. He shook his head and Clint struggled to explain.

"For starters, no kissing. Not on the mouth. Not on the neck. Nowhere. And no like, caressing or any familiar shit like that."

Jon jumped in to clarify. "He's basically saying, treat it like work. Even though you're going to be buried ten inches deep in the woman, be professional about it. It's a job. Not sex."

Ten inches? How the hell big was this guy? Mustang drew in a deep breath. "Um, okay."

Jon slapped him on the back. "Relax. This is the best job in the world. I wouldn't have been in the biz making seventy-five films a year for the last twenty years if it wasn't."

"Seventy-five a year?" Mustang looked at the man with new...respect wasn't the right word. Appreciation? Amazement? Shock?

"Yup. Do you know how much money that is?"

Mustang quickly did the math. During a good year, he made more riding bulls. He decided to keep that to himself and not brag, especially since he couldn't ride right now.

From the door of the barn, someone shouted, "Places. Five minutes."

He panicked. "I haven't seen the script yet. I don't know my lines. I don't even know the story."

Jon smiled and Mustang had a feeling he was amusing the man. "Here's your story. Arizona and I are supposed to be a married couple who own this ranch. We're getting busy in the barn. You walk in, say something like, 'I'm done with the chores' or something equally as cowboy-like. Then she tells you to come over and join us, which you do. Just follow our lead and the director's instructions from there."

"That's it?"

Clint laughed. "This isn't being made for the Academy of Motion Pictures, although the adult-film awards in Vegas last year was pretty kick-ass."

Jon shared Clint's amusement at Mustang's expense with a chuckle. Still grinning, he pulled the robe belt tighter one more time and turned toward the barn. "Come on. I'll show you where we're set up to shoot."

Mustang swallowed the lump in his throat. "Thanks."

In a flurry of activity Mustang was placed outside the door of the barn in the brilliant sunlight as both Jon and Arizona dropped their robes into the hands of a stage hand and without even a blink of an eye, strutted naked as the day they were born into the dimness of the barn.

He realized he was shaking like a leaf from head to toe when Missy yelled, "Action!"

It didn't get any better when just a few minutes later, after some sex noises came from inside the barn, someone poked him in the back. "You're on. Get in there."

After a moment of being absolutely frozen in place, Mustang got his body to move. Facing the rankest bull on the circuit paled in comparison to what he was about to do. He clamped his hat down lower on his head and entered the barn.

Blinded from the sun, he couldn't see a damn thing inside except for spots for a few seconds, even with the lights set up at just about every possible angle.

An unexpected cow's moo from one of the stalls had him jumping. Then he remembered he had a line. "Uh, ma'am. I finished my chores."

Good thing the dialogue—if you could call it that—wasn't anything more complex. He'd barely gotten that much out.

"Mmm and I see you've gotten nice and sweaty from them too." Arizona rose from her knees where she'd been occupied sucking Jon's insanely enormous cock.

Holy shit. Mustang began to feel inadequate. He was big, but damn, Jon could probably suck his own dick without even trying too hard, the thing was so long.

Then Arizona was there, unbuttoning his shirt. She pushed it roughly down off his shoulders. He tried not to cringe when she reached his forearm and her hand banged his tape-covered incision.

She went to work on his belt next. "Oh, what a big buckle you have. I hope what's underneath is equally as big."

He suspected that was a real-life warning. He better live up to her expectations or else. Mustang glanced again at Jon, who had just begun stroking himself while watching the two of them.

Sharing a woman with Slade or Chase, friends whom he knew well, was one thing. A threesome with this guy and his baseball-bat-sized dick in front of a crew and cameras was quite another. Mustang began to doubt his decision.

Arizona's hands slid his jeans and boxer shorts down over his hips. Then she was tugging on Junior with both hands. "Mmm. What do you have for me, big boy?"

He looked down to see he didn't have much of anything for her. Concentrating, Mustang willed his dick to get hard, but the harder he thought, the softer it became.

Moaning for the cameras, Arizona dropped to her knees and took what little of him there was at the moment into her mouth. Even that didn't help much. He moved to lean his hands on her shoulders so he wouldn't fall over, then stopped himself. He wasn't supposed to touch her, but damn, she was working him so hard, he almost lost his balance.

That would be all he needed, to fall over and re-break his arm while his jeans were down around his ankles. He probably shouldn't be thinking about broken bones if he wanted to get aroused. He tried to concentrate again, but then she dropped him like a hot potato and stood.

Spinning toward someone to the left of him, Arizona threw both hands up in the air. "He can't even get hard."

"Cut!"

The activity started again around him. Missy and Clint rushed to calm Arizona while Jon wandered over to Mustang. "You okay?"

Feeling exposed enough talking to a fully erect naked man, Mustang pulled his pants up so at least one of them was clothed. "I don't know if I can do this here, like this."

"I got something for you. Hang on." Butt-ass naked, Jon walked as confidently as if he'd been wearing a three-piece suit over to a small table set up in the corner of the barn. After wrapping a towel around his waist, he reached into a duffle bag, fiddled with something and then returned to Mustang.

"Here. Take this." Jon thrust a bottle of water and a small blue pill at him.

Mustang's eyes opened wide. "Is that..."

Jon looked around and lowered his voice. "Shh. Yeah. Just take it and don't tell anyone I gave it to you."

What the hell would Viagra do to a healthy young man who didn't—usually didn't—have trouble getting it up? Mustang guessed he'd find out. He swallowed the pill along with a mouthful of water. Just in time too, because Missy was suddenly next to him and nearly saw him taking it.

"What's the problem here, Mustang?"

"Give the kid a break, Missy. It's his first time," Jon defended him.

"Time is money, Jon. You know that. I can't have an entire crew sitting around waiting for him to get it up."

"I'm sorry." Mustang hung his head in shame.

"He'll be fine in a few minutes. He just needs to get used to it all. Right, buddy?" Jon slapped him on the back.

Mustang nodded. "Yeah. I think it's all the people watching."

Not to mention that Arizona was such a raving bitch. He wouldn't normally get within ten feet of her, forget about willingly fuck her. At least not sober.

Maybe he needed a drink to do this. Viagra and alcohol and whatever residual painkillers were still in his system, all before lunch. Mustang wondered how lethal that combo would be.

"I'll clear the set except for essential personnel. That's the best I can do for you. Get yourself together. You've got five minutes." With that, Missy exited, shouting orders as she left.

He glanced at Jon. "Will that pill work in five minutes?"

"No. You're going to have to help it along a little. You got a steady girlfriend, Mustang?"

"No." No way would he do this if he did. He didn't care how much they paid him.

"How about some hottie at home you've done or are hoping to do that you can imagine sucking you off instead of Arizona?"

Mustang's mouth felt dry, whether from nerves or the pill Jon had slipped him, he wasn't sure. He took another swallow of the water and considered the question. The image of Sage's heart-shaped lips wrapped around him immediately jumped to mind. "Yeah."

"Think about her then. If you can just get it up, the pill will do the rest and keep it up."

He drew in a shaky breath. "I think I need a little time alone."

Jon nodded. "You got it."

Mustang wandered outside. He probably was down to three of the five minutes he had been allowed to get it up. He sighed. Nothing like a little pressure.

A bull stood penned up not far from the barn. Mustang gravitated to the animal. Everything inside may be a different world to him, but this he knew. "Hey, big guy."

The bull raised his head, looking unconcerned. Most times if you left them alone in the field bulls were just big, lazy pets. It was when you forced them into a chute no bigger than they were, tightened that flank strap down and then jumped on their back with spurs on that they got pissy.

He hooked the heel of his boot on the bottom rail of the fence. "Did you ever have to service a particularly bitchy heifer and have trouble performing, my friend?"

The animal watched Mustang with a blank expression as if to say of course he didn't have trouble. He was a dumb beast and rutting was instinctual to him. Natural. Nothing to worry about. Too bad Mustang couldn't adopt the beast's attitude, at least for the next few hours anyway.

A few hours. Mustang kept that in mind. In a few hours he'd drive away from this place fifteen hundred dollars richer. He could go home and if things got really bad, he could tell his father he was quitting the prison.

Then tomorrow, after about three or four showers between

now and then to wash the porno feel off of him, he'd go pick up Sage and they'd spend some quality time together.

Picturing a picnic blanket on the grass by the lake, Mustang imagined a basket filled with Grams' tasty food and Sage, both laid out for the taking. She'd be in a little sundress that hid just enough and clung in all the right places.

He remembered how her mouth curved so easily into a smile whenever he joked with her. God, how he wanted to kiss those lips again.

Now he was glad he wasn't allowed to kiss Arizona in the movie. He may have to fuck the bitchy woman, but at least kissing would be something special he would do only with Sage. Even if he didn't let himself go any further than that with her, it would be enough.

He remembered the heat of her mouth from their kiss the other night. He imagined the feel of her body pressed against his. Warmth spread through him just at the thought.

Something began to stir down below. His hand dropped to the front of his jeans and he rubbed the growing bulge through the denim. How many times had he touched himself while thinking of Sage since he'd returned home? He couldn't even begin to count. She was his new favorite fantasy.

Remembering the feel of Arizona's mouth working him just moments ago, Mustang replaced her with Sage in his mind and rubbed harder. He wanted that so badly with Sage, but not just her mouth on him, he wanted to lay her back and push that sundress up so he could taste her too. Work her until she squirmed beneath his mouth and hands. When she begged him to stop he'd keep going, making her come over and over.

Mustang realized he could feel every beat of his heart throbbing in his cock. What all of Arizona's work hadn't accomplished, just thinking about Sage had. He was hard. Not just semi-hard like at the photographer's studio either. What he was sporting now was a full-blown, blue-veined diamond cutter to rival even Jon's equipment.

Mustang spun back toward the barn, taking off at a run. He cleared the doorway yanking at his jeans button and searching for Missy, or Arizona and Jon. "I'm ready. Let's go."

Jon grinned and dropped his towel. "Okay, then."

Arizona pursed her lips. "Now he's ready and we all have to jump?"

"Yes, we do. Time is money. Come on people. Get ready to roll." Missy clapped her hands and started shouting orders. "Mustang, drop those jeans again. Arizona, back on your knees. We're taking it right from where we left off."

Mustang did as he was told. Missy yelled, "Action!" and Arizona's mouth closed around him. He squeezed his eyes shut.

It's Sage. It's Sage. It's Sage.

He chanted the mantra and held on tightly to the fantasy as she took him deep into her throat. She moaned and it sent spine-tingling vibrations resonating straight through him. Her expert hands worked him along with her mouth. He took a wider stance, both to get better balance and to give her better access. She took advantage of that and began stroking his balls. They drew up against his body, tightening.

"Move your left hand, Mustang. It's blocking the shot."

As disruptive as nails on a chalkboard, Missy's order startled him, jerking him out of his fantasy world. He moved his hand and Arizona kept going but the fantasy world he'd created was shattered.

"Don't come in her mouth. We want a full-facial come shot. Okay?"

Mustang's eyes whipped open and he turned to look at

Missy. "Um, I don't think I can come yet." *Especially if you don't stop yelling orders at me.*

How long would it be before he could finish? He'd never taken pills for this before. Who the hell knew what it would do to him.

"That's fine. We'll shoot the money shot later. Let's move on to the threesome."

Arizona let his dick slide out of her mouth with an audible pop and turned to walk back to the blanket-covered bales of hay where Jon had been watching. Mustang realized a camera had been on Jon as well as them as he'd supposedly enjoyed the action between his on-screen wife and the hired ranch hand.

Mustang was handed a condom and told to put it on. At least they practiced safe sex. Something else he'd forgotten to ask before he'd agreed to do this.

Off to the side, Arizona was doing some stuff he'd, in all his years of being with women, never seen before. He tried not to stare before she caught him watching and raised hell. Instead, he sent a questioning look in Jon's direction.

"She's stretching her hole," Jon told him.

Mustang's jaw dropped. He stretched his muscles before a bull ride, but not that muscle and definitely not like she was doing.

Jon laughed. "Don't look so shocked. How do you think girls in these movies take all that stuff up their asses? Fists, dildos, bottles, huge cocks. You can put pretty much anything you want up there if you prepare properly."

He couldn't resist glancing over again. Arizona must have sufficiently stretched because she was heading their way.

Averting his gaze before she accused him of staring and

being a pervert, Mustang waited for the instructions he knew Missy would be bellowing at them soon.

He wondered where his place would be in this threesome. Considering the movie was called *The Double P*, he was pretty sure he knew what the choices would be.

A guy he hadn't noticed in the crowd before handed him a big bottle with a pump in it. "Lube up good, man".

After those instructions to *lube up good* and Arizona's preparations, he could guess where he'd be. It was his absolute favorite place to be inside a woman, but he wished he wasn't going to be inside this particular woman.

Mustang felt a little tingle run through him at the thought of what it would feel like to sink himself deeply inside Sage like that.

His naughty thoughts about her helped to keep him hard even though a strange guy was standing there impatiently waiting for him to lube his cock so he could take the bottle back. Mustang made short work of the job and handed off the lube, happy to send the guy away.

"Jon, I want you on your back. Arizona, kneel down in front of him. We'll start with you blowing Jon first while our cowboy here is in your ass. Mustang, come right up behind her but make sure the camera has a clear shot. We don't want to miss your entry." The fun began again when Missy started barking.

She was like a football coach and her team moved as instructed, like a well-oiled machine. Actually, they were literally oiled.

The camera moved so close he could hear it running. Arizona kneeled and thrust her ass up in front of him and Mustang came face-to-face with her stretched business end. He hesitated, trying to figure out what to do with his hands and worrying if holding on to her hips would constitute touching her too much or if Missy would yell he was blocking the shot.

Arizona's spun to shoot him a nasty look over her shoulder.

"Will you fuck my ass already before I have to go stretch again." Mumbling, she added, "Damn newbies."

Mustang's jaw tightened, his back teeth clenching until they went numb. "My pleasure, darlin'."

Nothing like a bitch to get a man mad enough to bring back his confidence. If she wanted it she'd get it, and he'd make sure she had nothing to complain to the boss about either.

Newbie, his sweet ass. This fucked-up business may be new to him, but he'd been fucking women for years. There were two things he did exceptionally well and this was one of them. He'd just let the insecurity and the situation get to him. Not any more.

Mustang slid in with one good thrust. He fucked her ass hard and fast until he heard her moan around Jon's cock in her throat. It wasn't one of those fake porno moans either. What he heard was the sound of a woman who was enjoying herself.

He felt himself getting close and decided to give Missy her money shot. Just before the point of no return he pulled out, yanked off the condom and came all over Arizona's lower back in messy, satisfying spurts.

Still hard from either adrenaline or the Viagra, he turned his head and found Missy behind him. "You want me to keep going?"

She smiled. "Get the man another condom and more lube. Can someone please clean off Arizona?"

He suited up again and the group moved under Missy's direction into one more position, the old double P with Jon on the bottom, Arizona straddling him and Mustang poised in his former position at the entrance to Arizona's ass, which definitely did not need stretching again after the fine job he'd just done.

As they all waited for Missy to yell action, Jon smiled in his direction. "You're doing good, kid."

Mustang laughed bitterly. "Thanks."

"You ever do this before?" Jon tipped his head to indicate the three of them and how he and Mustang would very shortly both be inside the same woman, separated by nothing more than a thin wall of membrane.

"Yeah. Quite a few times. No problem."

Jon raised an eyebrow. "Really? Humph. Who knew bull riders had such interesting sex lives."

He laughed. "Oh, man. You have no idea."

"You okay here?" Missy stuck her head close to them.

Mustang tried to ignore she'd basically directed her question to his dick. Since Junior couldn't answer her, he did. "Just fine. Ready to go whenever you are."

Jon laughed. "I'll work with this guy again whenever you want, Missy."

God help him. He probably would do this again. While he was laid up recuperating and couldn't ride, the money was too damn good not to.

"Good to know." She backed away. "All right. Action."

Mustang plunged again into Arizona, who didn't have anything nasty to say to him this time. With a great feeling of satisfaction that she had nothing to complain about after his performance, he held deep and waited until he felt Jon get himself positioned inside her too. Then Mustang went to town. If he was going to do something, he'd be damned if he didn't do it well.

At that thought, he finally got what Jon had been saying.

This had nothing to do with sex. This was a job. The question was, as much as he loved sex, did he want it to become a job? Mustang knew the answer without thinking anymore about it.

Definitely not, but what choice did he have?

Chapter Eleven

Sage leaned in and nipped at Mustang's lower lip in a way he normally would have loved. Not today. Instead, he felt like he needed to go shower—again—after what he'd done yesterday.

He shouldn't have agreed to meet Sage at the lake only twenty-four hours after he'd whored himself for money. He'd spent the entire day fucking a strange woman on camera and he really had thought he could pick right back up with Sage. It wasn't working out quite that easily.

Her tongue slipped between his lips and he tried to put aside thoughts of anything except her. Then Sage reached for his belt buckle and brought back the memory of Arizona's rough hands and mouth on him.

He took hold of her hand and stopped her.

"I want to." Her words were soft and sweet. The exact opposite of Arizona's angry, harsh tone yesterday.

He shook his head. "No, Little Bit."

"Stop calling me that. You do it every time we come close to doing anything more than kissing."

"We've done more than kissing." He remembered how she'd rubbed against him until they'd both almost come.

"Touching each other with all of our clothes on does not qualify as *more*." Her voice went from sounding almost angry to sad. "Why don't you want me?"

"I do. You have no idea."

"Then why don't you ever want to do more?"

Drawing in a deep breath, he rolled her over onto her back. "I want to do more. Believe me." Mustang watched her expression soften.

"Then take more."

Sitting up on his knees, he glanced around. The spot was secluded, but they were out in the open in broad daylight. Somehow that made it even more arousing for him. Judging from the expression on Sage's face, the setting was doing it for her too.

Sliding her sundress up her legs, he got his first unobstructed glimpse of her thighs. Gone were the scrawny chicken legs he remembered from their youth.

The sling was in his way so he took it off, tossing it to the side. Unencumbered now, he ran both hands over her curves, pushing the dress higher to expose plain cotton panties and finally, the satiny skin of her belly.

Sage reached and pushed the underwear down past her rounded hips slowly. He swallowed the lump from his throat and watched as more flesh came into view. He shouldn't have done it, but when the panties reached her knees, he slid them the rest of the way off, tossing them on the blanket next to them.

Then she spread her legs and everything was there in front of him, ready for the taking. He really wanted to take too. He'd spent most of the day yesterday fucking and yet he wanted Sage so badly now he was shaking.

He spread her lips with trembling hands and ran one finger lightly over her most sensitive spot. Sage's breath caught in her throat as her body jolted from that small touch. Mustang repeated the action and her eyes closed.

Her body, wet and welcoming, was so ready for him he could have buried himself inside her with no effort whatsoever. He'd promised himself he wouldn't do that. It was a hard promise to keep at the moment.

Dipping his head low, Mustang flicked his tongue against her clit. Her hips jerked beneath him. He worked her harder and got an equally satisfying response. She was close. It wouldn't take much to push her over. Then maybe they could, he didn't know, skip rocks on the lake or something. Anything so he wasn't tempted to take her.

He slid one finger inside and she moaned. Mustang pressed the sweet spot inside her while working her with the flat of his tongue and she cried out. Every response drove him a little more crazy. He only hoped he could stop from sliding into her when she came, which he knew would be any second as he felt her muscles tighten.

She exploded beneath him and he rode her orgasm out to the end until he was in agony from wanting her. He was so hard he throbbed. Needing to hide the temptation from his sight, he pulled her dress down after she'd finished shaking.

Flopping onto his back, he tried to regain his own breath and his resolve. Sage panted as she lay next to him, and Mustang concentrated on anything he could besides her in hopes his near-painful erection would go down.

He could still taste her on his tongue, hear her there next to him, feel the warmth of her thigh as it rested against his. He told himself he'd take care of himself later. Unfortunately, Junior wasn't buying the argument. Especially once Sage rolled over and started running a finger up his leg. He slapped his hand down to still hers.

She sat and crawled on top of him, straddling his legs.

"No, Sage," he said firmly.

"Yes." Ignoring his protest, she undid his belt and then lowered his zipper.

Admittedly, it wasn't like she could overpower him, even with his one arm not as strong as it should be. Yet he seemed unable to stop her.

He made one more attempt. "Please, Sage. Don't."

"Shh," she said while she lowered her head and pushed the waistband of his boxers down.

Feeling her breath on his cock, he shuddered. Then the hot wetness of her sweet mouth surrounded him and he knew he was going to let her do this. Worse, he really wanted her to.

Mustang gave up fighting with himself and watched the tip of his length disappear between her beautiful lips. She couldn't take him all in, but he didn't care. She looked up and his breath caught in his chest as he stared into her eyes.

She started to use both her hands and mouth, increasing the speed. As much as he wanted to watch, he couldn't keep his eyes open any longer. He threw his head back against the blanket and grabbed her face with both hands. He felt his balls tighten and he thrust up into her mouth. Holding her, he came deep in her throat.

Sage kept working him as his body jerked, sensitive to the point of pain. Drawing a sharp breath in between his teeth, he pulled her head away. Once free of her mouth, he tried to regain his wits.

The guilt hit when his brain did start to function again. At least they hadn't had full-blown intercourse. He hadn't quite broken his promise to himself about not having sex with her before he left. She gazed at him with an expression of complete satisfaction on her face and he groaned. He wanted her all over again. It was going to be a long few months.

Unable to look at her, he stared up at the sky. "You shouldn't have done that."

"I wanted to." He felt the weight of her head resting on his stomach.

"God help me, I wanted you to too."

"Then what's the problem?" He knew she was smiling even without looking. A content, sweet smile.

Once he left here, he'd planned on not looking back on his few months of purgatory. But now...

"You know nothing about me, Little Bit."

"I know lots about you. I always have."

He raised his head enough to see the determined expression on her face. She sat up. He saw the pinkness still in her cheeks from what they'd done. So sweet. So innocent. So not ready to hear his confession about having sex with another woman on camera, no matter what the reason.

He pushed himself up with his good arm. Standing, he reached down to help her. With guilt lying in his gut like a rock, he scooped her panties off the ground and handed them to her, unable to meet her eyes as he did.

"Come on, I'll walk you home. I'll get the food basket. Can you grab the blanket?"

Her face showed the doubts he knew he'd caused in her. He'd messed things up thinking with his dick again. Maybe one day he'd learn to stop doing that.

As she stood waiting with the blanket in her hand, he grabbed her face and planted a quick hard kiss on her lips. He pulled away and stared hard into her eyes. "I'm no good for you, Sage."

A devilish look appeared in her smile. "Maybe that's why I like you."

Mustang laughed. Maybe it was.

Mustang's head swirled with thoughts of Sage as he walked home alone after dropping her off. Then he saw his father's truck parked in the driveway and his mixed feelings about the last few hours were replaced with dread about another workweek looming just hours away.

He was so deep into his misery thinking about work that the sound of the phone ringing in his pocket made him jump.

"Hello?"

"I've got another movie for you, if you're interested."

Mustang gripped the phone tighter. Interested? No. Desperate? Pretty much. The fifteen hundred he'd earned wasn't enough to ensure he could pay his bills for possibly four months. And what if he got back on a bull and couldn't ride? He'd have to keep working with his father.

That thought made his decision. "The same kinda set up?"

"Not exactly. I know you said last time you're only interested in movies where you can keep your face mostly covered and off camera. This one is perfect for you, but it's for a niche audience."

What the hell did that mean?

"But the pay is more because of that," Missy continued.

More than fifteen hundred? "How much more?"

"Two thousand."

Shit, now he was very interested. "For one day?"

"Yes, for one day, but I have to tell you it's for the BDSM

market."

"You mean whips and stuff?"

"Mmm hmm. Among other things."

Mustang didn't know if he could whip a woman, even if he was only pretending for the cameras, but two thousand dollars...

Remembering how he'd neglected to ask the proper questions last time, he decided to not make the same mistake again. He considered what else he wanted to know about this gig. "Would it be with Arizona again?"

Considering how she'd treated him last time, he could probably get into whipping Arizona.

"Nope. We have a girl who does all our BDSM films. Mistress Lena. Ever heard of her?"

Mustang smothered a laugh at the name. "No. Sorry."

"She's good at what she does. Lena will be able to lead you through, no problem. So you game?"

Mustang stifled some more guilt. The only woman he wanted to be with was Sage. The one woman he shouldn't be with was also Sage. Meanwhile, he was about to agree to fuck another stranger for money.

It's not sex. It's a job. Jon had said that and Mustang did his best to believe it. Clint and Arizona felt the same as Jon, judging by the whole division between boyfriend-sex and work-sex thing.

Two thousand dollars. Mustang glanced down at his bum arm that still had months of healing to go before he could ride.

"Yeah, I'm game."

Chapter Twelve

"Here's your mask."

Mustang took the black item in his hand, frowning at the object that looked more like part of a superhero costume than something used for bondage.

It would cover his face nicely. He guessed that was the most important part.

The guy handed him a pair of black vinyl pants next. "And these are for you to put on."

That was it. The man's hands were empty. "No shirt?"

"Nope."

Mustang's incision was still very visible, but he'd protected it with clear surgical tape again. Since Missy hadn't mentioned it being a problem last time, he didn't think he'd have to worry today.

He looked around him. This shoot was in what he could only call a mansion, judging by the huge columns outside, the marble-floored foyer bigger than half his parents' house and the sweeping staircase leading up to an open second-floor hall lined with doors.

"Where should I change?" The guy's eyebrows shot up and Mustang guessed that even though they were standing in the foyer, it had been a stupid question. "Here, I guess?"

"Yeah. Here is fine." Missy's assistant pointed to a table against the wall. "You can leave your stuff over there. We'll be filming here in the foyer."

"All right. When do I get my whip and stuff?" He kind of wanted to get a feel of it before the cameras started rolling.

"Lena's the only one that touches the whips." The guy laughed at him. "She's the dominatrix. You're the sex slave. You didn't know?"

"Um, no. I guess I didn't ask."

"Oh, man. Are you in for a hell of a day." He walked away still chuckling.

She handled the whips. It sure explained why he wasn't given a shirt. Unbuckling his belt, Mustang began an internal pep talk to calm himself. How bad could it be? He could handle pain. He was a bull rider for God's sake. Besides, she wouldn't really hurt him. This was all for show. He could handle it.

Feeling better, he dropped his jeans and unfolded the black pants...and things got a little bit worse. He held them up and inspected them more closely and yeah, he was right, there was no ass and no crotch.

Maybe his back wasn't going to be the only thing getting whipped today. Shit.

He pulled on the pants, feeling like an idiot with his business hanging out and then feeling even stupider trying to tie the mask around the back of his head.

"Need some help with that, sugar?"

A woman dressed all in black leather, right down to the thigh-high boots, and carrying a whip sauntered up to him. Mistress Lena, he presumed.

"Yeah. Thanks." He held up his left arm. "I had surgery a few weeks ago and it's still a little stiff."

"No problem." She put down the whip and came up behind him, taking the mask and making quick work of tying it on. "That's done. Now let's see what else I can make a little stiff besides your arm, shall we?"

She smacked his bare ass with the flat of her open palm hard enough to cause a pretty good sting. His brows shot up in surprise. She was flirting with him? What happened to the this-is-a-job-not-sex rule?

Lena couldn't have been more different from Arizona and he wasn't sure he liked it.

"You ready to get started?"

"I haven't been told my lines yet."

"You don't talk, except to answer if I ask you a question. Like if I say, 'Call me mistress', you answer, 'Yes, mistress'. It's easy. You'll get the hang of it. And if you mess up, that's okay too. It'll just play into the scene."

"I guess I'm ready then."

"Great. Missy, we're ready, hon. I just need the rest of my stuff brought in."

Missy appeared. "You heard her. We're ready. Someone get Lena her stuff. Places."

Lights flipped on, blinding him. "You get over by the stairs, sugar. On your knees on the bottom step, your arms braced a few steps up."

Oh boy. Mustang swallowed hard. "Okay."

He kneeled, realizing the position left him totally out there for all the world to see when he felt the cool air hit his balls.

"Action!"

Lena launched into her lines, something about how he'd been a bad boy and needed a spanking. Then she proceeded to give him that spanking until he was sure his flesh was as red as a baboon's ass.

"I think you like the spanking. Do you like the spanking?"

Uh oh. Time for his line. "Yes?"

"Yes, what?" she shouted, accompanying the question with another slap.

"Yes, mistress."

"Louder!"

"Yes, mistress!"

She took out the whip she'd hung on her belt and started belting him with that while she talked more about his need for punishment, most of which he didn't pay too much attention to as he wondered what kind of people got off watching this stuff. His mind was wandering when suddenly, the whipping stopped and he felt something cold and wet press against his anus.

Mustang jumped and spun his head to look back at her. "What are you doing?"

While he watched, she took another dollop of lubricant from a jar someone must have handed her off camera.

"I'm teaching you a lesson. Don't question me." Lena pushed his shoulder until he was facing the steps again and couldn't watch what he feared was about to happen. He sure felt it though as she slowly pushed her finger deep inside him. "Do you like that?"

"No, mistress."

She laughed. "I think you do. I think you're lying, and lying needs to be punished."

Her finger withdrew and returned, feeling slicker than before. She added a second finger and his muscles tightened against the invasion. It didn't stop her. Instead, she pumped them in and out a few times and then left him totally. He dared to turn his head to see what she was doing, not daring to hope this part was over and she'd go back to whipping him.

He wished he hadn't looked when he saw her lubricating the handle of the whip. He swallowed hard and watched in horror. For the first time he took a good look at her whip and realized the handle was shaped just like a penis.

It was a big handle and he had a bad feeling she was about to stick it in a very small place while he could do nothing but kneel there helplessly with his lubricated ass waiting in the air for her. His heart pounded so hard he could feel it vibrating his throat.

Now he knew what the extra five hundred dollars in his pay was for. It must be the anal-intrusion bonus. He considered yelling "cut" himself and leaving. How angry would Missy be? Considering the number of crew and the amount it must have cost her to rent this place for the day, he figured she'd be pretty angry. Plus he'd signed some papers when he'd arrived. He probably should have read those. She could most likely sue him for breach of contract or something.

Lena kept talking, but he couldn't concentrate on anything else besides his fear of what was to come. This was only the first scene. He was here for the whole day. Holy crap. What else would they do to him?

It was too late. Mustang had to go through with whatever Lena had planned. He swallowed hard and decided it might be best if he didn't see what was happening. Pressing his forehead against the step in front of him, he closed his eyes and drew in an unsteady breath, praying it would all be over soon, just as Lena pressed that big, slick cock-shaped whip handle against him and pushed.

Mustang's cell phone rang during the drive home. He really didn't want to talk to anyone. Every time he moved his butt in the seat the soreness reminded him of what had happened that day.

A ringing phone was hard to ignore, but he managed it. He didn't even glance at the caller ID. If it were Sage he would have been tempted to answer it. He couldn't talk to her right now. Not when he couldn't even face what Lena had done to him with that big, phallic whip handle.

He'd never had anything up there. Ever. One woman had ventured near the area with her fingertip once while they were fucking and he'd shut that plan down right away.

Yet for money he'd let Lena stick not only her fingers in him, but push that obscene-looking thing deep inside. Lena was nothing if not patient and thorough. Oh, yeah. She'd taken her time sliding it in and out of him agonizingly slowly. Over and over while she talked some nonsense and slapped his ass cheek. He couldn't comprehend anything she said. He'd simply knelt there, his head pressed against the cool marble step, and felt that thing push past muscles he knew he should try to relax but couldn't.

Push and withdraw. In and out. Every time she pulled it out he prayed it would be the last time. When it finally was, what happened next was worse.

Lena strapped on a harness, complete with a frighteningly life-like dildo, lubed up until it glistened. She'd made him face her, his knees against his chest. After the size of the whip handle, the smaller, flesh-colored cock had slipped easily inside him. Like his body was made for it. He felt the blood rush to his face just remembering that.

What Jon had told him the week before didn't help the situation or make him feel any better about it. *You can fit pretty much anything up there if you prepare.*

She'd grabbed his hips and thrust into him like he was the woman and she was the man. Then he'd gotten aroused. Not just partially, but a full-tilt, point-to-the-sky erection.

Mustang couldn't even conceive of that. He knew for a fact he wasn't gay. He loved sex with women above all else. So why did Lena sliding that thing that looked like a man's dick into his ass get him hard? Not just hard either. When she'd ordered that he make himself come, he'd stroked himself barely a dozen times and, beyond all comprehension, he'd shot off like a rocket.

While she pressed that thing deep inside him, he'd come with one of the most intense orgasms he'd ever experienced. What the hell did that say about him?

The phone rang again and this time he couldn't ignore it. Anything was better than reliving the scenes from today, so he picked it up and pushed the button for speakerphone. "Hello."

"Hey. You haven't called since right after your operation. We were worried. How are you?" Jenna's familiar voice filled the cab of the truck.

"I'm okay. The arm's healing. I can use it pretty much. I'm actually driving right now."

"You're driving? Mustang. It's bad enough you're driving with one broken arm. You shouldn't be talking on the phone too."

"Jenna. He's a big boy. Leave the man alone." Slade's muted voice came through the phone.

"You're there with Slade?" He hadn't noticed how much he'd missed them both until he'd heard their voices again.

"Yeah. I've kinda been traveling with him the last two weeks."

Mustang could see he wasn't exactly being missed by his best friend. He guessed he couldn't blame them for taking the time to be alone together.

His mind flashed back to some of the stuff he, Slade and Jenna had done together and he couldn't resist asking her about what was uppermost in his mind. "Um, Jenna. Can I ask you something personal?"

She laughed. "Yeah, sure. I suppose so."

It was a silly question considering their past together, which is exactly what made her the perfect person to ask. "When we were all together. When you, uh, came with uh, me in your ass, was it much more intense than usual?"

There was a moment of silence before she finally said, "Of all the possible questions I could have imagined you asking, that was probably the last one I would have ever come up with. And the answer is yes, incredibly intense. Should I bother to question why you needed to know that?"

He sighed and regretted asking immediately. He'd just been trying to find an explanation for what he'd felt today.

"No reason. Just wondering," he lied.

"Hey, Slade, I think there may be a girl in Mustang's life." Jenna's voice got softer as she must have pulled the phone away from her mouth to report back to Slade.

Slade, sounding muted, answered her. "There are hundreds of girls in Mustang's life, sweetie."

Mustang shook his head. *Nice friend.* "Hey, Jenna. Tell Slade thanks a lot for me."

She laughed. "You want to tell me about her and prove Slade wrong?"

"There's nothing to tell." Not about Sage, who he couldn't let be his girl since he was leaving. Definitely not about Lena, who he hoped to drink out of his memory later that night. And Arizona he'd pretty much forgotten about already.

"Hmmm. Methinks the man doth protest too much."

"Yeah, yeah. You writers and your fancy talk." Mustang smiled. It was good to talk to his friends again, even if he was in hell at the moment.

"Well, I'll let you go so you can concentrate on the road. Do you remember how to put more minutes on the phone when you need them?"

Mustang rolled his eyes. "Yes."

"Call if you need anything, okay?"

"Yes, Jenna."

"Take care."

"I will. You and Slade too. Bye." He disconnected the call just as he pulled onto his parents' road.

When he'd first heard he'd be making two thousand dollars for the day he'd considered telling his father to take his job and shove it. He'd thought if he did need more money he'd just make another movie. Now he knew he couldn't go back to doing that kind of movie ever again, no matter how much he needed the money. He couldn't give up the job at the prison just yet. Besides, the dread of telling his father he wanted to quit nearly equaled the dreadful memories of Lena.

Mustang had been through enough already for one day.

Chapter Thirteen

Sage glanced at the clock in the corner of her computer screen. Seven-thirty and Mustang still hadn't returned her call after she'd left him a voicemail hours ago.

She debated whether to call again, then talked herself out it. How pitiful would she look? Calling a guy over and over again when he didn't call her back. Especially a guy like Mustang.

She had yet to discover where he'd disappeared to for two Saturdays in a row. He was always so vague when she hinted around for information.

Scrubbing her hands over her face in sheer frustration, she pushed the chair back from the desk. She got so crazy thinking about him she could barely sit still in her seat. She thought of him day and night, remembering the roughness of his hands on her bare skin. The heat of his tongue on her.

She couldn't concentrate on schoolwork. Her mind kept going back to the too few times she and Mustang had been alone together and how he avoided having actual sex with her no matter how much she hinted. If taking off her underwear and laying herself out like a picnic on the blanket didn't tell him she was ready and willing, what would?

This whole thing was confusing.

Maybe she was crazy for wanting him. Wanting to have sex with the town bad boy she'd loved since puberty while knowing he was leaving town again in a few months was insane.

Sage was so deep in her thoughts her phone ringing made her jump.

Mustang.

She flung herself forward to grab the cell phone lying on the desk and answered it.

"Hey, Little Bit. Sorry I didn't call sooner. I just figured out now how to get your message off my phone." The voice that made her tingle inside filled her ear.

He sounded weary. Whatever mysterious errand he'd gone on today must have been really strenuous.

"That's okay." She'd only spent a few hours in self-imposed agony. No big deal.

"You said something in your message about a plan?"

Sage had wracked her brain for an excuse to be alone with him again and had finally come up with the perfect one. Well, maybe not perfect, but it was something.

"The bull-riding competition is on television tonight. I remember you saying you don't have a TV in your bedroom there and I figured your parents wouldn't watch it in the living room, so I thought you might want to come over here and watch it with me." *In my room. On my bed.*

She was babbling. She knew that. But that's what Mustang did to her sometimes. Especially lately. It was like she was a twelve-year-old with dorky glasses and braces all over again.

Sage thought she'd die waiting for him to answer, but finally he did. "Okay. I'll be over in a little while."

"Great. See you soon." Flipping the phone closed, she dropped it on the desk and sprung into action. She had to straighten the room and change clothes.

What the hell should she wear? She'd better brush her

teeth too. With any luck, there'd be kissing, and hopefully much more.

Maybe she should put new sheets on the bed. Then again, what was she thinking? Her grandmother was home. Kissing was one thing, but doing anything more was quite another. Particularly the one thing she really wanted to do with Mustang.

She had just finished up in the bathroom and was checking her reflection in the mirror when she heard voices in the kitchen.

"Thanks, Grams. I'm good. I ate dinner at home." Mustang's voice grew louder as he came down the hallway toward her room.

Letting out a long, steadying breath, Sage tried to strike a pose that looked casual. No, she hadn't just flown around like a maniac getting ready for his arrival. She always lounged around her room at night wearing lip gloss and a flirty sundress that provided easy access to her brand new lacey panties, should anyone be interested in gaining access.

Sure.

She had it bad. Sage shook her head at how pitiful she was just as Mustang appeared in the open doorway. He raised a fist and rapped his knuckles softy on the wood frame. "Knock, knock."

"Hey." Her voice sounded breathy in her own ears. "Come on in. Um, I think it's starting soon. I guess I should turn on the TV and find the right channel."

He dipped his head in agreement and walked in, glancing around the room. His gaze went from the bed to the one chair.

"You can get comfortable. The best view of the television is from the bed." If he sat in her desk chair she'd never have a chance of attacking him.

142

"Okay." He perched on the edge of the bed, his boots still on the floor as he sat up straight with his back against the headboard. He looked uncomfortable but at least he was on the bed where she could sit next to him.

Sage heard the television out in the living room, loud and in Spanish, and knew her grandmother had settled into her chair for the night where she'd most likely fall asleep.

Rosemary used to sneak boys into her room after their grandmother had gone to sleep all the time. Sage tried to remember that as she felt guilty about plotting on how best to seduce Mustang under her grandmother's roof.

She remembered the purpose of his visit and turned on her own TV, grabbing the remote control off the top and carrying it back to the bed. She perched on the other side of the bed, but since it was a twin-size they were still pretty close. For the first time in recent years she was happy the mattress was so narrow.

Finding the right channel, she turned the volume up just enough that they could hear it and set the remote on the bed table. "It looks like it just started."

"Yup."

He was in a strange mood. "You look tired."

"A little." Mustang shrugged. "Long day."

Sage jumped on the chance. "Yeah? What did you do?"

"Work."

Hmm. A one-word answer. It must have been a really bad day. Sage groaned in commiseration. "You have a bad drive with your dad?"

"No. Different work." His short answers told her he didn't want to talk about it.

"Oh. Okay." Sage folded her hands in her lap and pretended to care about what was happening on screen.

She heard Mustang sigh and then his arm was around her shoulder. Luckily, he'd sat on the side that put the good arm, the one not in the sling, next to her.

Sage glanced sideways at Mustang and he answered her unspoken question. "I think I could use a hug."

Mustang Jackson, the mighty bull rider, asking for a hug. Even in the old days when his father had taken a switch to him for something he'd done, or possibly hadn't done, he'd never asked anyone for a hug. Not Rosemary or Grams or her. Something was definitely up. Her gaze met his.

"Lucky for you, I'm good at giving hugs."

Still looking sad, he managed a crooked, half-smile. "I know."

As she leaned into his arm, he tipped his head down, brushing her forehead with his lips. Tilting her head up, she touched her lips to his chin, then kissed her way to the corner of his mouth. Mustang hesitated but it didn't take any more coaxing before his lips met hers full-on.

In mid-kiss, he pulled away. "Your grandmother."

"She's settled in front of her programs. We won't see her for the rest of the night."

He drew in a deep breath and then he was kissing her again. This time deeper and with more energy. He didn't seem tired anymore. Mustang only stopped kissing her long enough to slip the sling off his neck. His hand came up to cup her breast. He ran a thumb over her nipple through the fabric of her dress. She felt it harden under his touch.

She groaned then broke away. "Is your arm okay?"

"Arm? What arm?" He lowered his head to trail kisses along her neck.

He pushed the top of her dress down with her bra and took

her nipple between his lips, torturing her with his teeth and tongue.

Eyes closed, Sage leaned back against the pillows, memorizing every sensation that shot through her. His mouth sent electrical current straight through every part of her body. She wanted more.

Sage guided her hand on a path up Mustang's thigh toward the long, hard bulge straining the zipper. She'd tasted him, felt what it was like to have the length of him in her mouth. She wanted it elsewhere.

She stroked him through his jeans and he moaned, letting her breast pop out of his mouth.

"We're not going any further than this." The warning sounded stern and definite, until she stroked him again, harder. He closed his eyes and drew in a shaky breath. "You are going to be the death of me, woman."

"Mmm, but it will be a fun way to go." Smiling, Sage took advantage of his weakening defenses. She felt for the tab of his zipper until his hand clamped down over hers.

"You are a determined little thing, aren't you?" He chuckled.

It was nice to hear him laugh, even if he wasn't letting her have her way. Maybe the subtle approach didn't work on Mustang. Steeling her nerves, Sage gathered her courage. "I want you."

"I want you too, Sage, but we can't always have what we want."

She tried to move her hand to touch him again, but he held her firmly.

"Why won't you make love to me?"

He laughed. "Besides the fact your grandmother is in the

next room?"

Sage felt the pout form on her lips. "But even at the lake you wouldn't."

Mustang drew in a deep breath. "I told you. I'm no good for you."

"I don't care."

He brought her hand to his lips and kissed it. "I know you don't and I'm a bad enough man to take advantage of that."

She scowled. "You haven't taken advantage of me." Not nearly as much as she would have liked him to.

"Yeah, I have. I've selfishly convinced myself that what we're doing is okay as long as that's as far as it goes."

"Ah. The Bill-Clinton definition of sexual relations. As long as it's not actual intercourse it doesn't count." She let out a snort as she finally understood Mustang's plan and his reluctance to have sex with her.

He laughed. "Yeah, I guess something like that."

Sage shook her head. "I hate to tell you, Mustang, but just because we haven't, you know, doesn't mean what we've done isn't sex."

The expression on his face grew serious.

"You're right." Mustang pulled his arm from around her shoulders. "That's why we have to stop doing anything at all."

Oh, no. That wasn't the result she had been looking for. "What? No. That's why we should just go for it and go all the way."

"No." Mustang shook his head.

"You can't put the spilled milk back in the carton, Mustang. We've already done a whole bunch of things. Stopping now won't change what happened." She folded her arms and frowned.

146

He laughed, tapping her lips with his fingertip.

"You are adorable when you pout." He sighed. "But you're right about the milk. We sure have spilt a whole bunch. How about we just go back to doing what we were before?"

"Okay. For now."

Hoping he was referring to the kissing and orgasms and not watching television, she inched her hand up his thigh. Laughing, he pulled her close again with one arm around her shoulder. "I can feel your hand on my zipper again, Little Bit. I told you no."

He'd caught her red-handed. "But we've already done that, so it's allowed."

Mustang lowered his voice. "Even so, I'm not going to sit here in your bedroom with my dick out and your grandmother in the living room."

"Fine. Be that way." Sage crossed her arms again.

Laughing, Mustang's hand moved down and began a journey up the inside of her bare leg. "Maybe I could make it up to you in some way."

"Maybe." She continued to scowl, but moved her legs wider as he dipped his finger beneath the edge of her panties. He moved, smooth and sure, right to where she needed him to be, zeroing in on her most sensitive spot.

Her moan caught in her throat and she closed her eyes. Sage raised her hips off the bed as he circled his finger. She pressed harder against his hand but it wasn't enough.

She let out a groan of frustration and then felt his breath warm against her face. "What's wrong, darlin'?"

"More."

Chuckling, Mustang slid a finger inside and started to perform his special magic. A small sound escaped her.

"Better?" Hearing the self-satisfied smile in his voice, she didn't answer. Instead, she reached up and pulled his lips down to meet hers as her body started to shake. He groaned against her mouth as she came.

She never wanted the moment to end. Eventually the orgasm did end, but the kissing continued until he pulled away suddenly and sat up.

"What's wrong?"

He shushed her softly, all of his attention on the television across the room. He stood and moved closer to the set.

Pushing her dress back down her legs, she got up too and walked over to where he stood next to the television.

She saw what had Mustang's attention and a lump formed in her throat. She pushed the button on the front of the set to raise the volume.

An announcer's voice filled her room. "Skeeter's glove is still caught up in his rope. The bull fighters are trying to get him loose but Six String is not slowing down."

She watched in horror as what looked more like a rag doll than a man got tossed and dragged by the giant bull.

"Come on," Mustang whispered. "Fuck. The rope won't release. Dammit, Skeeter."

He ran a hand through his hair, shaking his head.

The bull and rider were finally separated, which only allowed the bull to turn and more effectively tromp on the rider's motionless body on the ground. A bunch of men jumped in, grabbing the bull by the horns, smacking it in the ass, anything to draw its attention away from the rider, which was the sole center of its attention.

A horse and rider appeared on screen, throwing a rope around the bull's horns to help get him away from the injured man. Finally the bull was chased out of the arena as the announcer kept up his running commentary.

"The sports medicine team is with Skeeter. You never can tell at this point how bad the injuries are."

The camera's zoomed in closer and Sage watched the motionless, crumpled figure on the ground with horror. The packed arena was as silent as her bedroom as everyone waited. A stretcher was brought out and the station cut to a commercial.

Mustang had his cell phone out and was pushing buttons. "Slade. What's happening with Skeeter? The damn station cut it off."

He began to pace the room, alternately talking and listening. Sage stayed out of his way until he finally disconnected the call. "How is he?"

"They don't know yet. He's unconscious. They want to move him to the hospital but his back could be broken so they gotta be careful. Fuck. It's my fault."

She frowned and stepped closer to him. "How can it be your fault?"

"Skeeter asked me to show him how to do a suicide wrap and I did." He let out a bitter laugh. "How stupid. I should have said no. Dammit. It's called a *suicide* wrap, for God's sake. What the hell was I thinking?"

Sage had watched enough bull riding over the years to know what he was talking about. "Lots of riders use that wrap."

"Yeah, but I didn't teach it to them." Mustang shook his head again.

Coverage of the event came back on and Sage and Mustang stayed glued to the television until his cell phone rang. He whipped it out and answered. "Slade. What'd you find out?"

Mustang listened for a bit and then let out a shaky breath. "Damn. Keep me updated. Okay? Thanks." He closed the phone and she waited. "It looks like it's not a broken back but they're not sure how bad the internal injuries are. He's in the hospital now. He was conscious for a little bit, but he was really out of it."

"Thank God he at least woke up."

Exhaustion marred his face. "Yeah. Look, I hate to leave, I mean after..." He glanced at the bed. "I'm not going to be good company right now. I think I should go."

Sage nodded, hiding her disappointment that he didn't want her comfort. "Okay."

"You sure?"

What was she supposed to say? *No, it's not okay that you're upset and leaving because your friend is in the hospital and you think it's your fault.* His need to be alone was bigger than her selfishly wanting his company. As much as she wanted Mustang to let her comfort him, she had to understand that. "Yeah, I'm sure. I'm here if you need me. I mean day or night. You know that, right?"

He nodded. "Yeah, I do." Mustang leaned in and, brushing her cheek with his hand, kissed her forehead. "Night."

"Night." Sage watched him leave her room and sighed. He was a loner and probably always would be. Silly her for hoping she could make him into anything else.

Chapter Fourteen

The ringing of his cell phone woke Mustang out of a fitful sleep. He found himself flat on his back lying crossways on his bed with the lights and his clothes both still on.

He fumbled for the phone and finally got it open. "'lo?"

"Hey, it's Slade."

"Slade. How's Skeeter?" Mustang frowned at the clock on the dresser. It was just after eleven p.m. He must have passed out the minute his head hit the mattress a few hours ago.

"We haven't heard anything more from the hospital yet, but I'm about to go crash for the night. I wanted to let you know. I'll call you in the morning when I find out what's up."

"Okay. Thanks, man." Mustang's brain started to fire again as he slowly woke. "Hey, you guys are heading back out west next, right?"

"Yup. Guthrie, Oklahoma and then Weatherford, Texas. Thinking about driving out?"

"Yeah, actually I am. I'll call and let you know."

"It's convenient having a cell phone, isn't it?"

Mustang heard the smugness in Slade's voice. "Yeah, yeah. Night, Slade."

"Night, man."

He disconnected and rubbed a hand over his face.

Mustang kept thinking about the worst-case scenario, about what could have happened. What if Skeeter had been paralyzed in that crash? That would be a fate worse than death to Mustang. Even though Skeeter wasn't paralyzed, it still didn't mean his riding career wasn't over.

Seeing Skeeter's wreck had been an eye-opener. What if Mustang got injured again and couldn't ride anymore? A steady job with a regular paycheck and benefits, even one at the prison with his father, might look pretty good.

Shit. He was starting to sound like his father.

Wide awake now, he glanced at the clock again. No way was he falling back to sleep anytime soon. He felt like he'd crawl out of his skin if he didn't get out of this tiny room and move around.

He grabbed his keys off the dresser and then crept past his parents' bedroom. He left through the back door, not sure where he was heading, just that he had to get out of there for a bit.

A few minutes later, he found himself parked and staring at the dark silhouette of Sage's house. She had said she'd be there for him whenever he needed her, day or night. He needed her now.

Walking quietly to the side of the house so he didn't wake her grandmother, Mustang reached up and tapped on the glass of her window. Gently at first, then louder when she didn't come.

Finally, he saw the curtains move and her face appeared. She raised the window and leaned down. "Mustang. Is everything all right?"

No. Everything was upside down and nothing made sense anymore. "Yeah. Can you come out and talk?"

She didn't hesitate. "Sure. Just let me throw shorts and

shoes on. I'll be right there."

He nodded, realizing coming here to Sage now was the stupidest thing he'd done in recent memory. Then he remembered how he'd spent most of that day with Mistress Lena doing the unthinkable and revised that opinion.

The kitchen screen door squeaked and Sage appeared wearing an oversized T-shirt that he bet she slept in, shorts and flip flops.

She came right to him and wrapped her arms around his waist. "You okay?"

Not strong enough to fight it any longer, he pulled her close and held tight. "No. They still don't know exactly how bad Skeeter is."

"I'm sorry."

He glanced up at the house and realized how close they were. "Maybe we should go talk in the trailer before we wake up Grams."

"Okay."

The nearly full moon lit the way to the trailer. Mustang opened the door for Sage, letting her climb up into the living area before he followed her inside. He turned on a small battery-operated light that cast a soft illumination over the interior.

She stood next to the bed and looked around before turning back and watching him, waiting for him to talk, he supposed. Unfortunately, seeing her there and given his current mood, talking was the last thing he needed.

"Sage." He took a step closer and touched her face. Her expression told him she wouldn't say no, no matter what he asked of her. "I'm not sticking around here any longer than I have to."

"I know and I'm okay with it."

Marveling at her, he shook his head. "Why the hell would you want to get involved with someone like me?"

She shrugged. "I can't seem to help myself."

He lowered his head and hovered near her lips. "Neither can I. I promised myself I wouldn't let things go any further with you, but dammit, Sage. Life is too damn short. What happened to Skeeter tonight could easily happen to me."

Her finger came up and rested against his lips. "Shh. Stop talking and make love to me."

Sage kicked off her shoes and shorts, then raised the T-shirt over her head and dropped it on the floor. She'd been wearing no bra or panties. She stood naked in front of him.

A groan of pure defeat rumbled deep in this throat. He ran both hands down her exposed curves, shivering right along with her when his thumbs brushed her nipples on the trip down.

Her hands began to work on his belt and he let her. He lowered his head and took her mouth with his while her fingers found first his zipper and then the erection behind it. She reached inside his underwear and stroked him while he groaned against her mouth.

"I've waited too long for you already, Mustang Jackson. Take off your boots and clothes and let's get in that bed."

Who was he to argue? He did as he was told, stopping only to grab condoms and lubricant out of the drawer. He lay back on the bed and Sage crawled on top, straddling his legs.

She reached for the condoms and he stopped her hand. "Wait. You won't be ready yet."

Sage laughed. "I'm ready. Believe me."

Mustang shook his head. She didn't understand. He was big. Not as big as Jon Long, but still. And Sage was young and he doubted very experienced. That thought didn't help his guilt any, but as evidenced by the erection jutting straight up between them, it hadn't dampened his need for her any.

"No, Little Bit. I don't want to hurt you."

"If you call me Little Bit one more time, I'll hurt you. Now let me put this thing on you." She held up the condom, threatening him with it.

He laughed at her determination.

"Okay, but please use the lube, Sage. I really don't want to hurt... Ah, holy mother." He didn't have the time or wits to finish the sentence because Sage had already sheathed him and had begun to lower herself over him.

His eyes slammed shut and his head hit the mattress as he felt her body start to engulf his. He finally forced his lids open enough to be able to watch his length disappearing slowly inside Sage.

"You okay?" His voice sounded strange to his own ears.

She drew in a sharp breath as he sunk deeper. "Yes."

"I don't want to hurt you."

"I won't break. I promise." Leaning down, she brushed a gentle kiss across his lips and lowered herself a bit more onto his cock.

He held her still with one hand on each of her hips. "I know, but tell me if I..."

"Mustang. Shut up and make love to me. Unless of course, you don't know how."

He laughed. It was different being with a woman he knew. *Really* knew. "I know how."

"Then you better prove it."

Loosening his grip on her, Mustang stopped fighting. He let Sage work until he was fully seated inside her. She set a slow pace that had him shivering each time she raised herself up and then slid back down. He watched her face and her gaze never left his.

This was more than sex. Much more.

Not prepared for the intensity of what he'd feel with Sage, Mustang sought to do the one thing he was familiar with. Please her.

He found her clit with his thumb and then the pace she set wasn't so slow anymore.

In a frenzy of motion, he knew he couldn't last much longer. When she cried out and he felt her body gripping him, he came right after her with a soul-shaking release he hadn't felt in a long time, if ever.

Breathless, Sage collapsed onto his sweat-drenched chest. "Once isn't going to be enough."

Still inside her and in shock at the connection he'd felt between them, Mustang had to agree.

The distant ringing of his cell phone woke Mustang about dawn. Sage was sprawled across him. Two discarded condom wrappers lay next to his hand on the bed. Memories of round two the night before had his body waking up in a very obvious way. That would have to wait.

His phone was somewhere on the floor in his jeans but how he was going to get to it with Sage on top of him, he didn't know.

Mustang worked his way from beneath her. She moaned and rolled over from the disruption, curling up into the fetal position. Hugging his pillow, she went right back to sleep so he didn't feel too bad. However, the phone stopped ringing long before he made it to his crumpled jeans and found it in his pocket.

It took him a minute to locate the missed calls, but before long he'd hit the right buttons and was listening to the ringing through the line. Glancing at the bed and Sage's peacefully sleeping figure, Mustang closed himself into the tiny bathroom. He had to pee anyway.

Finally, Slade answered.

"Hey, Slade. Sorry I missed your call. What's happening?"

"No, I'm sorry. It's way too early on a Sunday morning for you to be up, but I thought you'd want to know what was happening. We got word on Skeeter. He's got a lacerated liver, contusions in both lungs and fractured ribs. He's still in the hospital. The docs say he'll most likely be out for three to six months."

"Damn, but still, thank God it wasn't worse." Three to six months out of competition, but at least it hadn't been a career-ending injury. After watching that crash and the sports medicine team's reaction to it, Mustang hadn't been so sure. Skeeter was bad, but it was a relief it wasn't worse. Everything would heal. He'd been lucky...this time.

He blew out a long, slow breath. "Thanks for telling me, man."

"No problem."

Mustang said goodbye and hung up with Slade, took care of business in the bathroom and then wandered back to the bed. It was too early to be awake. Unfortunately, he'd have to rouse Sage and sneak her back into the house.

If her grandmother woke up and found her missing, she would most likely look outside, see his trailer and know her granddaughter wasn't missing at all. She was just getting busy with Mustang. The last thing he needed was Grams, the woman who had watched him grow up, knowing he had taken advantage of her granddaughter.

He crawled back onto the bed and nestled up close behind Sage so he could wake her up slowly. The problem was, Junior didn't wake slowly. He'd gone down nicely during the phone call, but now he detected Sage's warm, naked body and sprung to life. Pressed close against the crevice of her ass, Mustang was starting to lose incentive to send her home.

When she moaned softly and nuzzled against him, all sense fled. His hand crept over her hip and snuck between her thighs. Another sleepy, happy sound rumbled from within Sage and she bent one knee, giving him total access. Sadly, he took full advantage. He began circling her clit with his finger as his erection teased her.

The discovery that she was already wet had him groaning. He let just the tip of his cock slip inside and his eyes squeezed shut at the sensation. She pushed back and he slid in farther. He worked his hand faster and her hips began to move. Before he knew it, he was thrusting fully inside her. Her muscles began to pulse around him and he pumped harder.

She cried out as she came and Mustang felt the tingle begin inside him. He sank into her one last time, intent on finishing deep within her, and then he realized what he'd done. Pushing Sage forward, he yanked himself out just as he came all over the sheets.

"Holy crap." He let out a shaky breath over the close call. "I can't believe what I just did."

Sage rolled bonelessly over, lying on her back next to him. "What's wrong?"

"I forgot the condom. I can't believe it. I've never done that before, Sage. Ever. I mean I pulled out, but still, I didn't even realize what I'd done until it was almost too late."

"But it wasn't too late, so it's okay."

He shook his head. "It almost wasn't."

"Are you sorry that we made love?" She watched him closely, waiting for an answer.

He cupped her face. "No, I'm not sorry but I'm damn pissed at myself for being stupid."

No woman had ever made him forget himself the way he just had with Sage.

His forgetfulness with Sage was proof that one day in the future, either by choice or by accident, he may need a steady job with health benefits and a pension plan and that meant the end of his career. That scared the hell out of him. His head was starting to hurt.

Sage broke into his thoughts. "You weren't stupid. Now stop. Everything is fine. Let's change the subject. What do you want to do this weekend?"

"I was thinking about taking a road trip to see Slade and the guys in Oklahoma. Stay and watch the competition."

"Oh? That sounds like fun."

Mustang could be dense at times, but this wasn't one of them. Sage was waiting for him to invite her to go with him.

How the hell could he do that? Jenna was still traveling with Slade. Chances were good that their past together could come out. Though he didn't want to lie to Sage, he also didn't think she could handle that revelation.

Then there was Chase, who could easily trot up and start running off at the mouth about his and Mustang's recent threesome.

He felt enough like the devil on earth when compared to Sage and she didn't even know a fraction of what he'd done in his life. Yes, it was before they'd gotten together, but still.

She quietly waited for him to say something. He felt horrible about it, but he needed to get out of taking her with him somehow.

"Um, I'd invite you along but I'm going to spend the whole time catching up with the guys, and Slade always used to stay in the trailer with me..."

Sage laughed. "Yeah. That would be a little crowded. The three of us in this tiny trailer."

He'd had more than three people in his bed a time or two. Tamping down the guilt, Mustang let out a breath. "Exactly. You understand, right?"

"Of course, but I'll miss you." She nipped gently at his chin with her teeth.

"I'll miss you too, Little Bit." Running his hand up her body, Mustang leaned his head down. His lips hovered tantalizingly above hers and then he thought better of it. With a groan, he leaned away. "I better not start something we don't have time to finish."

Quickies just weren't possible with Sage. He found he never wanted his time with her to end, which is why he tried not to think about the day it would. Maybe that was another reason to not quit the prison. Working there would make Mustang's remaining weeks in Magnolia feel like an eternity.

Sage sighed and rolled off the bed. "I better get home before Grams wakes up. When are you leaving for Oklahoma?"

"Right after work Friday, I suppose."

"I guess we won't have much time together before you leave since you have to work all week." She sounded sad as she pulled on her shorts.

"I'll be home Sunday night." Regretfully watching her tug the T-shirt over her head, covering the last of her beautiful, exposed nakedness, Mustang rose from the bed himself.

"You better be good while you're gone." She stood on tiptoe and kissed him on the mouth.

"I will." As if he had a choice. He hadn't even thought about another woman since that first night he'd seen Sage at his parents' house. After the time they'd spent together, he wasn't sure he'd ever be able to *not* think about her again.

"No hopping on a bull to see if your arm is better." Her eyes narrowed with warning.

He laughed. She hadn't been talking about other women at all. "No hopping on any bulls. I promise."

"Okay." She hovered in the doorway of the trailer. "See you."

"See you, Little Bit."

Watching her roll her eyes at the name and disappear down the stairs, he realized he was in big trouble. He missed her already.

Chapter Fifteen

After hauling ass for most of the trip, Mustang pulled into the parking lot of the arena at about eleven o'clock Friday night. He got out of the cab with a groan, stretching muscles stiff from sitting in one position for too many hours.

He hadn't stopped, just driven straight through. Now he could use a rare hamburger and a cold beer. A men's room would be handy too. Luckily, he knew where he could find all that and more.

The neon beacon across the street beckoned. Slade and Jenna had called about an hour ago. They'd pulled into town earlier that night and checked into the hotel. They should already be at the bar waiting for him. When he pushed through the door and heard Jenna's squeal, he knew they were.

"You made it." She jumped up from her chair.

"Yup. I made it, darlin'." Mustang accepted her hug, before shaking Slade's hand and eyeing his beer on the table. "Hey, man. It's good to see you. Damn, I could sure use one of those."

Slade laughed. "I bet. I'll get you one."

Jenna grabbed his arm. "Wait. Are you still on painkillers? You can't drink if you are."

Mustang smiled. "No, mother. I'm not on the pain pills."

He would have been tempted to lie to her even if he was

still taking them. Luckily, he was done with pills, until the next injury, at least.

Slade paused, brow raised. "Am I allowed to get him a beer?"

"Yes." Jenna narrowed her eyes. As Slade headed for the bar, she added, "Smart ass."

Mustang laughed. "Uh oh. Is there trouble in paradise?"

"Nah. We're good. We just spend a *lot* of time together. When you're on the road it's twenty-four seven."

"Tell me about it. I've been traveling from one end of the country to the other with him for much longer than you have."

"I know. How did you two never kill each other?" Jenna shook her head in amazement.

Two bottles in hand, Slade walked over just at that moment. Mustang accepted the beer and raised it in salute to Jenna. "Alcohol helps."

Jenna lifted her own drink in a toast to Mustang, sent an innocent glance at Slade and took a long swallow.

Mustang smiled. "I've really missed you guys. Tell me everything that's happened since I've been gone. How's Skeeter?"

"Not too bad. He says he'll be back next season."

"I'm glad of that."

Jenna leaned one elbow on the table. "You tell us what's been happening with you. How's it being home?"

Slade cringed at Jenna's innocent question. "You probably shouldn't bring that up."

"Why?" She looked from Slade to him.

"I'm not a big fan of visiting home, is all. No big deal." Mustang explained.

"But why don't you like going home? With you guys being on the road so much, I'd think being home would be a nice change."

Mustang laughed. "You haven't met my father."

Realization crossed Jenna's face. "Ah. Hey, did you stop to eat during the drive? I think the kitchen's still open."

"Yeah, I could eat, but wait one minute. You, the inquisitive writer who has a question for everything, is willing to let the subject about why I don't like going home drop? Just like that?"

Jenna shrugged. "No need. I totally understand."

Still confused, Mustang looked to Slade for an answer.

"Mother issues," Slade supplied.

It seemed these two really had gotten to know each other living together on the road. There was definitely a story there and Mustang wasn't sure he was up to hearing it right now. "Listen, I need to hit the head. If a waitress wanders by, order me a burger rare and fries."

"You got it." Slade nodded.

Mustang returned to the table moments later and found a place setting, a bottle of ketchup and a fresh beer had been left at his seat. Things were looking up.

Until Jenna started talking again. "So, who's the girl?"

He frowned and glanced around the bar. "Which girl?"

"The one at home you're not telling us about."

"What makes you think there's a girl?" He tried to keep his face neutral.

"For starters, there's a bimbo leaning against the bar with her boobs ninety percent out of her top and you haven't even glanced at her."

"That's because I'm too busy looking at you, darlin'." He

grinned at her and let his gaze drop suggestively down her body.

"Bull shit. You didn't even try to kiss me or cop a feel when I hugged you. There's a girl." Jenna narrowed her eyes at him.

Mustang looked helplessly at Slade, who just laughed. "Sorry. You're on your own there, buddy. I already have my hands full with her."

"What's that supposed to mean?" Jenna's unhappy gaze redirected in Slade's direction.

Slade scowled in Mustang's direction. "See. Now you've got me in trouble."

Mustang laughed. "You did that all on your own, man. Don't blame me."

The burger and fries arrived and life was good. Slade and Jenna were providing his dining entertainment. His blissfully parent-free accommodation for the night was parked conveniently across the street. What else could a man ask for? All right, maybe Sage in his bed tonight would be nice. And his name on that rider board for tomorrow too, now that he thought about it.

He bit into the burger and the juices flooded his mouth. For now, this was good enough.

"Damn." Jenna suddenly reached into her ever-present sack of a purse that seemed to follow her everywhere.

Mustang wiped his mouth with the napkin. "What's wrong?"

"I forgot I was supposed to email my agent with that list of dates and cities where Slade'll be riding."

Mustang's gaze swung to Slade. "Why?"

Slade rolled his eyes. "They're going to plan a bunch of book events around the tour."

Whipping the tiniest computer he'd ever seen out of her purse, Jenna set it on the table and flipped it open. "It's brilliant. I mean, the book is about bull riders, right? So what could be better than having book signings at the events?"

Mustang's eyes opened wide. "Like inside the arena?"

"Out in the lobbies, probably. In some locations they'll be bookstores located pretty close to the event but mostly, yeah, at the arenas."

"But, uh, then won't people figure out that, uh, you know...it's us?"

Their threesome was the subject of that damn romance novel Jenna had written. Pretty much every detail from what he'd read.

Jenna glanced up at him. "I've found there are generally two types of people. Those who believe the author has personally done every single one of the things they write about, no matter how kinky or absurd the story, and those who think everything is fake even when it's absolutely real."

"Uh, yeah, but Jenna." He lowered his voice. "We really did do all that stuff in your book."

Normally, at least a few months ago, Mustang wouldn't care who knew what had happened in Tulsa. That was before Sage had come into the picture.

"What I'm saying is it doesn't matter whether we did or didn't. People will believe what they want anyway, so I'm not worried." She shrugged.

With a glance at Slade, who echoed Jenna's shrug, Mustang let out a long breath. "Okay. If you say so."

Jenna clicked around on her tiny contraption for a few minutes. Then she typed so fast he could barely see her fingers, before she flipped the lid shut.

He frowned. "What did you just do?"

"I emailed the event list to my agent."

"You can get on Internet sites and stuff with that little thing?"

"Yeah. Cool, huh?"

He nodded. "Could I, uh, get on a website?"

Slade's beer halted halfway to his mouth. "You. On the Internet?"

Mustang scowled at his comment.

Jenna smiled. "Maybe he wants to email his girlfriend."

"I wouldn't know how if I wanted to," Mustang admitted.

Jenna's eyes opened wide. "Ah, ha. So there is a girl. Here you go. It's all yours."

Slade laughed as Jenna passed Mustang the computer. He took one look at it and slid it back to her. "I'm not emailing anyone. I just wanted to check something. Could you do it for me? I want to see if this site is up yet."

Pulling his wallet out of his pants, he took out Guy's card.

She read it. "Sports Photography?"

He tried to play it cool. "Yeah, this guy had talked to some of the rookies about modeling for his site. I thought I'd check it out for them."

No way was he going to tell her or Slade about the nude modeling or the other stuff. Although, if this website was up and running and Junior was front and center, he may have to. He hadn't thought of that before he'd handed the info over to Jenna and her heightened curiosity. Shit.

"Sure, I can check for you." Jenna clicked around a bit and then shook her head. "Nope. It says it's coming soon."

"It doesn't say when it'll be up?"

"No. Wait a second though. Let me see something." Frowning determinedly at the screen, she started with the fast typing again.

"What are you doing?"

"I'm researching who owns the domain name and seeing if they have any other sites up."

He wasn't sure what all that meant and he wasn't sure he liked it anyway. When Jenna's eyes opened wide and she said, "Holy crap," Mustang knew for sure. He should have kept his mouth shut.

"What's wrong?"

"Mustang, this guy runs male soft-porn sites." Her shocked gaze focused on him.

Uh, oh.

"I guess it's a good thing none of those guys agreed to model for him then, huh?" He really wished she would close that thing. Reaching over, he tried to push the lid shut. "Thanks for checking. I'll let them know."

"Some of this stuff is really...wow." She smacked his hand away and kept clicking keys and he started to panic.

Slade's brows shot up to his hairline. "If it's so bad, Jenna, then maybe you shouldn't be looking at it."

"I didn't say it was bad." She grinned as Slade frowned. Then she paused and leaned closer to the screen, before looking at Mustang with her mouth hanging open.

He swallowed hard. "Um, what?"

She spun the screen to face him and there he was, in almost-full glory. "That's what."

He shook his head. "I don't know what you're talking about. And stop showing me naked men. I don't want to see that shit."

Flipping the lid shut, he hoped that was the end of it, but

she simply opened it again and there he was.

"What's going on?" Slade asked.

Mustang watched horrified as she spun the screen to Slade. He paled and averted his eyes immediately. "Jeez, Jenna. I don't want to see that shit either."

"Look closer." She demanded. "Don't you recognize those chaps and that hat?"

Slade forced his eyes back to the screen and then did a double take. "Holy shit."

"Look even closer and there's a fresh scar on his left arm, right about where Mustang's would be. Then there's his...you know."

Slade challenged her. "What about his 'you know'?"

"Well, I mean, I'd recognize that... Never mind."

Mustang felt his face growing warm. "Okay. It's me. They were paying a hundred and fifty an hour and I didn't know I'd be naked when I called."

"They didn't tell you?"

"Well yeah, on the phone they did, but they said it was artistic nudity. I figured... I don't know what I thought but I didn't think this."

She continued to stare as the screen until Mustang started to feel pretty uncomfortable. Then she frowned and clicked one more time and the reaction on her face told him he better look too.

Another page came up. In the picture, his eyes were closed as he grasped Junior in his hand and tugged, trying to get himself hard for the next shot like the photographer had requested, concentrating so hard he didn't know the damn guy was snapping away the whole time.

"Shit."

Then he noticed another man behind him in the photo. He was seated in a chair and enthusiastically jerking off while appearing to watch Mustang doing the same.

"Holy crap. Who the hell is that? I swear to you, there wasn't anyone else in that room except the photographer and me." Not like that made it any better, but still, he'd only done that in front of one guy and for the camera, not for that other guy to get off on.

Jenna leaned closer. "He's superimposed. It's a pretty crappy job but it looks real enough at first glance."

Slade leaned over and looked too, before quickly leaning back. "Damn. I told you I would have loaned you the money. You didn't have to do that."

He drew in a deep breath, thinking of what else he'd done rather than borrow Slade's money. "I know."

Then another thought hit him. The photographer knew Missy Love. He was the one that recommended Mustang for the job. What if the two sites were linked somehow? He swallowed hard. "There isn't any more on there, is there?"

If there was, Jenna and her writer's snooping abilities would find it. Better Jenna than Sage. God, how would Sage react if she knew? He couldn't even think about it.

Jenna clicked around some more. "No, I don't see any more, but that raises a very good question. What else could have been on there? What else did you do, Mustang?"

She leaned back and folded her arms and he knew he wasn't getting out of there until he'd confessed. He raised his arm. "Waitress. Another round."

Shortly thereafter Jenna sat wide-eyed and, amazingly, speechless. Meanwhile, Slade covered his eyes with his hand as he leaned his head heavily on the arm he had braced on the table.

Mustang swallowed the dry from his throat. He'd gotten pretty graphic. Knowing Jenna, she'd be able to find the damn videos anyway with a little research. He figured he better prepare Slade for that discovery.

"So, that's it. I've got thirty-five hundred dollars from the movies, thirty-eight if you count the uh, *modeling.* Looking back, I'd return every red cent if I could take back what I did to earn it."

Jenna frowned. "That's what I don't get though. You pride yourself on your sexual prowess."

That term had Slade laughing but she continued anyway. "Why are you embarrassed?"

He might as well come clean about it all. These two people were his closest friends in the world, not counting Sage, and that was complicated. "Because you're right. There is a girl and I don't know what she'll do if she finds out what I've done. She knows I posed nude, but that's it."

Mustang went on to briefly describe his relationship with Sage, both past and present.

When he was done, Jenna looked smugly at Slade. "Told you there was a girl."

Slade rose. "Yes, you did. I gotta hit the head. I've been holding it since he started this story. I didn't want to miss anything."

She watched him go all the way to the men's room, obviously proud of her powers of deduction. When he disappeared through the swinging door, she turned back to Mustang. "I'm sure everything will be okay. I mean, we only found it because we were looking."

"I know, but it feels really shitty lying to her. Keeping things from her. You know?"

"Wow. You really are serious about this girl. You must be. You didn't even suggest we go back to your trailer. I think you're in love."

Mustang sobered and let the idea sink in for a bit.

Maybe he was. That was some heavy shit.

Jenna laughed. "Don't look so miserable. I'm happy for you. I'm glad that you met someone special. Aren't you?"

"Yeah, I am." He let out a bitter laugh. "I think." What he wasn't so happy about was the idea of going back out on the road and leaving her. He sighed and then changed the subject. "So, are you planning on traveling with Slade for the rest of the season?"

She shook her head. "No, I'm heading back to New York after this leg of the tour. They're heading to the West Coast next and I have things at home I need to take care of."

Her face visibly saddened.

"You're gonna miss him."

She drew in a deep breath. "Yeah."

Mustang and Jenna were sitting in the silence of shared misery when Slade returned. "Why do you both look so serious all of a sudden?"

Jenna snapped out of her reverie. "No reason, but back to Mustang's situation. I think you need to tell her. If you feel strongly about her and you think you might have a future together, you can't start off with a lie."

Slade's head swiveled, telling Mustang he disagreed. "Nope. Keep your mouth shut, man. What she doesn't know can't get you in trouble. Chances are she'll never find out anyway. She doesn't sound like the type to be out renting pornos."

Jenna spun to face Slade. "You would start a relationship by keeping things from each other?"

This was one dogfight Mustang was staying out of. He took another swallow of beer and watched the action in silence.

"I'm saying if the truth would hurt her and it won't change a thing if she knew anyway, why tell?"

Jenna's brows shot up. "Oh, really."

"Look, Jenna. If I had gone and took a job that required me to have sex with other women before we started seriously dating, would you really want to know? Especially if I never was going to do it again?" Slade asked.

"Yes, I would."

That had been a silly question on Slade's part. Even Mustang knew the answer to that one. Of course, she would. Jenna had been bitten by the curiosity bug. She had to know everything.

Mustang couldn't be silent any longer and jumped in. "Okay, Jenna, I agree that you think you'd want to know, but the real question is would you be able to accept it? Could you get over it, forgive him and move on like nothing had ever happened?"

She sat for a second thinking and then shook her head. "I can't picture Slade doing that so it's hard to imagine."

"But you can picture me doing it?" Mustang scowled, not sure if he'd just been insulted.

"You did do it," she reminded.

"Then let's pick another scenario. Let's say Slade started seeing another woman back home in Texas after meeting you in Tulsa but before you met back up in New York. If after getting back together with you he vowed to never see her again, would you still want to know?"

"That doesn't work either." Jenna let out a sigh. "I know you were both seeing other women after Tulsa. If 'seeing' is really the euphemism you'd like to use for what you were doing."

"That's really what you think?" Slade frowned. "That I was with other women that whole time?"

Jenna nodded. "I try not to think about it, but really, we had no commitment. You guys were such playboys and then when you never called me. What was I supposed to think?"

Slade shot a nasty look at Mustang. This conversation wasn't going as planned.

"I didn't, you know. 'See' or do anything else with another woman while we were apart after Tulsa." Slade reached out and held Jenna's hand.

Her face softened. "You didn't?"

"No, I didn't." Slade shook his head.

"Aww. I didn't see any other men either." Her voice sounded all soft and lovey-dovey.

Mustang rolled his eyes. "Um, excuse me. Now that we've got that settled, can we get back to my problem?"

The two lovebirds continued staring into each other's eyes until Mustang leaned forward and tapped Jenna's forearm.

"How about this? Let's say Slade had been with someone else after meeting back up with you in New York." Before he got Slade in trouble, Mustang added quickly, "He wasn't by the way, but if he had been would you be able to forgive and forget?"

She frowned. "No, because that would mean he would have cheated on me after we agreed to not see anyone else. But that's not a good hypothetical situation unless you and this woman agreed to have a monogamous relationship before you made the videos. Did you?"

He shook his head. "Hell no. I wouldn't have agreed to the

movies if I had. I hadn't even had sex with her yet when I took the jobs. I'm not going to take on any more movies now that we are together like that."

"So then you weren't cheating on her."

"No."

"Then technically she really can't get mad at you," Jenna reasoned.

Slade let out a puff of air. Mustang glanced at him. "What do you think, Slade?"

"Whether she can or can't technically get mad at you, I still can't believe you're even considering confessing everything. I told you. If you're not going to do it again, keep your mouth shut."

Jenna gave Slade an unhappy look. "I really think we need to talk about this propensity you have for keeping secrets."

"How come I always get into trouble because of you?" Slade asked Mustang.

He couldn't worry about those two. Mustang had his own issues. Drawing in a deep breath, he looked at Jenna. She was all for him confessing his sins even though he knew her well enough to believe she'd be the first one to hold a grudge, no matter what she said. He glanced at Slade, who shook his head to reinforce his opinion against telling Sage anything.

"Okay. I'm not telling her." Mustang sat back, but that decision grated on his conscious. He leaned forward again. "But maybe she would understand. She knows what my father's like and how much I hate my job at the prison. Hell, I don't know."

Slade shook his head. "You are really fucked, man."

Didn't he know it.

Chapter Sixteen

"Mmm. I missed you."

"I missed you too, Little Bit." Mustang moved the hair from her neck and sent shivers down her spine when he kissed the sensitive skin just below her ear.

Sage's breath caught in her throat as he nipped with his teeth and then soothed it with a brush of his lips.

"Oh, really? Then why did you avoid me all week since you've been back?" She tried to make it sound like she was teasing, but the question was totally valid.

It would be easy to simply sink into the pleasure and forget her feelings. For her own sanity, she couldn't let that happen. Mustang had returned from Oklahoma late Sunday night and then had said he was too tired to see her every night during the week.

"I'm here now, aren't I?" Did he hesitate before answering or was she being paranoid?

They were only together now because she hadn't been able to stand it anymore and had walked to his house right after dinner. He'd made some excuse to his parents about taking her into town for ice cream, when in reality they were in the trailer parked behind some trees by the lake.

The scenarios running through her head for the past few

days as to why he was avoiding her had spanned some crazy territory. She imagined everything from his having met and become involved with another woman while he was away, to his having a secret wife and kids living in Oklahoma.

"Yes, you're here. Finally." She was starting to sound like a bitch.

He moved his hand to the button at the waist of her shorts. "Perhaps I can make it up to you."

He slid his hand into her panties and had her shaking in mere minutes. Then he stripped her bare and shed his own clothes. Donning a condom like he'd been appointed the poster boy for birth control after that one time he'd forgotten, he slid inside. He continued stroking in and out of her until they both gasped for breath.

Lying exhausted on his bed, Sage knew she was addicted to Mustang and the withdrawal was going to be bad. Too bad there wasn't any rehab for this kind of addiction.

Mustang's cell phone rang and he reached for his jeans on the floor. He frowned at the display. "I should take this. One second, Little Bit."

He held up one finger and, turning his back to her, he wandered over to the other end of the trailer. She could only hear half the conversation and even less than that once he disappeared into the bathroom, but from what she could determine, he was telling someone he was busy this weekend.

She wondered who exactly he'd be busy with. When he came back to the bed and flung the phone on the mattress next to him, she fought the urge to ask anything about the conversation.

Unfortunately, she lost the fight. "So, you have plans this weekend?"

Now that the sex was over, her mind had gone back to work

on making her insane.

Looking devilish, he dragged the tip of one finger down her stomach. "Why? Do you have something in mind?"

"That depends on if you're too tired or not." That came out sounding snippy.

He cocked one brow. "Oh really?"

She refused to give in to the distraction when he slid his hands between her thighs and instead kept her legs firmly clamped shut...until he began kissing a trail down her stomach. The lower his mouth got, the more her resolve lessoned, until she couldn't resist anymore.

He spread her legs easily enough once she stopped fighting. "I'm not tired now."

Grinning, he dipped his head low and she suddenly couldn't remember what they'd been talking about.

An hour later, when they were reduced to two tangled, sweaty bodies, Mustang groaned. "I have to get up."

"Why?" She rolled onto his chest and touched the cleft in his chin.

"I have to use the bathroom. Let me get up, get cleaned up, then I'll come right back. I promise."

With a moan of protest, she let him up but didn't resist watching his ass muscles move as he walked to the bathroom. The door had just closed when she heard a muffled sound coming from the tangle of blankets. Mustang's phone was ringing.

Sage knew the right thing to do would be ignore it and tell him it had rung when he got back. She could yell to him and ask if he wanted her to answer it. Or she could give in to morbid curiosity and look at the caller ID.

Leaping at the origin of the noise, she pawed through the

blanket until she found the phone just as it stopped ringing. But before the display changed to say *Missed Call*, it very clearly read *Jenna*.

The bathroom door opened and she dropped the phone, bunching the covers back over it. Shaking, she tried her best to look casual but one thing kept invading her mind.

Who the hell was Jenna?

Mustang crawled onto the bed and gathered her in his arms. She stiffened.

"I think I better go."

He sighed. "Yeah, I guess you're right. It's late. Your grandmother will start to worry. I'll drive you."

"I can walk."

"Don't be silly, Little Bit. My parents think I drove you into town. Of course, I'd drive you home too."

She doubted he called who ever this Jenna was by some silly nickname that made her sound ten years old.

Suddenly feeling sick, Sage swallowed hard, torn between asking him who she was and grabbing her clothes and running to find somewhere private to throw up.

"Okay," she whispered. "Thanks."

"Thanks a lot for calling me back, Mustang."

"What?" He barely recognized Jenna's sarcasm in his sleepy state.

"I called last night and left a message. You never called me back."

Mustang wiped a hand over his face and glanced at the bedside clock. It was too damn early for a lecture. "I'm sorry. I

179

didn't see a message. What's up? Why are you up so ungodly early on a Saturday morning?"

Jenna laughed. "Up late last night, were we?"

"Maybe." He'd been *up*, all right. Twice to be exact, which was actually fewer times than he'd like to be when he was with Sage.

"Anyway. We decided to stop by for a visit."

"What?" That woke Mustang up. He bolted upright. "You're coming here?"

"Yup. We've got a map that shows us how to get to Magnolia but we need to know where to go from there once we hit town. Slade doesn't have a GPS and he refuses to let me buy him one."

"Put Slade on the phone please, Jenna."

"He's driving."

"Please, just put him on."

He heard the transfer of the phone and then Slade's voice. "I told her you wouldn't welcome us with open arms."

"Jeez, Slade. What the hell? You don't call first?"

"She called last night. You didn't answer."

"Where are you coming from?" Mustang tried to remember the tour schedule but that part of his life had taken a back burner lately to all the rest.

"We've got this weekend off so I brought Jenna home to meet my father. She's been in my ear about coming to see you all week."

"You withstood it for a week. You couldn't last a little longer?"

Slade chuckled. "You don't know what she did to convince me."

Mustang could only imagine. He heard a slap and an "ow" from Slade. "You deserved that, man."

"Yeah, I guess so. Anyway, we're here now so tell us where to go."

"Go to the diner on Main Street and I'll meet you there." He was hungry now that he was fully awake and keeping Slade and Jenna in town would also keep them away from Sage and his father, which was a good thing.

They hung up and he threw clothes on. His mother was already up making coffee, but he bypassed that and headed for the door, telling her some friends were in town. That was followed by the usual invitation for them to visit, which Mustang dodged with some excuse as he grabbed his keys and escaped.

So far, so good. Now, if only Jenna would get her fill quickly and he could happily send them back to Slade's father.

Not long later, Mustang sat across from Jenna and Slade, a steaming cup of coffee in his hand and a scowl on his face. "So, Miss Curiosity, why exactly are you here?"

"To see you, silly." She had the innocent look down pat.

He let his gaze roam down her and noticed she still dressed like she was in New York, even when she was in a hole in the wall like Magnolia, Texas. "I don't believe you, darlin'."

"Why else would we be here?"

"You want to check her out."

Jenna tried to control her smile. "Who?"

"You know very well who. You may be able to wrap Slade around your finger with whatever kinky little thing you used on him, but it won't work on me." Then he thought about it. "Hmm. Unless you'd like to give it a try on me and see if it will work. What was it anyway?"

He looked from Jenna to Slade.

"Wouldn't you like to know," Jenna challenged. "Besides, it was for book research anyway. Getting Slade to do what I wanted and come visit you because of it was just a nice bonus."

"I was book research?" Slade frowned.

She shrugged. "Sorry, baby."

Mustang raised a brow. "Tell me when this book releases, okay?"

Jenna laughed. "I'll send you a signed copy."

Slade groaned and signaled for more coffee while Jenna leaned forward. "So, when do we get to meet her?"

He looked up at the ceiling. "Um, let me see. Uh, never?"

A frown furrowed Jenna's brow. "Oh, come on. What possible harm could it do?"

"Darlin', I couldn't even begin to list all the harm her meeting you could do." He pictured that cozy introduction.

Sage, this is Slade and his girlfriend, Jenna. She's the woman we shared for a week in Tulsa. You should read her book. It tells all about it, right down to the old double P. Yeah, right. He might as well add, *Oh, and by the way, that's the name of the porno I starred in too.*

He shook his head more adamantly. "Nope."

"There's a good chance we'll accidentally run into her you know."

"How would that happen when you're leaving right after breakfast?"

"Oh, didn't I tell you? We stopped by the hotel on the edge of town. They have plenty of availability in case we decide to spend the night." Jenna's grin was more evil than anything Mustang had ever seen.

He turned to his supposed friend. "Slade, come on. Help me out here."

Slade shook his head. "She's got a mind of her own, man."

"What'd she do? Threaten to cut you off if you don't do whatever she wants?" Mustang suggested.

Sipping at his coffee, Slade nodded. "That and more."

"If you just introduce us I'll be happy, and then Slade will be happy too."

"You're missing one thing, darlin'. I don't really care if Slade is happy." Mustang was scoring a victory for himself when his phone rang. Pulling it out, he took one look at the caller ID and debated. Finally, he flipped it open. "Hey, Missy."

"Missy? I thought he said her name was Sage." Jenna hissed to Slade.

Slade motioned for Jenna to hush up, and gratefully she did so Mustang could deal with this.

"Hey there, my star. I know you said you were busy today, but I could really use you on set. Jon's the star and he specifically requested to work with you again."

"Yeah, about that. I couldn't really talk when you called last night but the deal is, I'm not going to be, uh, taking on any more work in that area."

Jenna's eyes opened wide as she caught on. Slade took another second until she mouthed to him the word porno.

Mustang dragged his attention back to Missy's voice. "I'm really sorry to hear that. The camera loves you, Mustang."

Well, he didn't love the camera, or, come to think of it, a dick-shaped whip handle in his ass. "Thanks, but it's not for me."

"We could talk money if that's the issue."

"Nope, that's not the problem, but thanks for the offer."

She sighed deeply. "Okay. You'll call me if you change your mind?"

"Yes, ma'am." God willing he'd never need to.

"Oh, and I'd thought you'd like to know *Double P Ranch* is already on sale and *Mistress Lena's Punishment Part XII* will be out next week."

He felt his face heat and seriously hoped Missy's voice hadn't carried across the table to Jenna or Slade. He didn't need to be answering any questions about what his punishment had been in graphic detail. That was the one specific he'd left out of his confession. Some things a man couldn't tell even his best friend. "Great. Thanks for telling me, Missy. Good luck today and say hey to Jon for me."

"Will do. If you change your mind we'll be back at the ranch where *Double P* was filmed."

"I don't think I will, but thanks."

The table was strangely silent. Two sets of eyes focused solely on Mustang as he flipped the phone shut.

"Wow." Jenna let out a long, slow breath. "I know you told us about the videos, but hearing even half that phone call made it seem even more real."

She should only know how real it felt being the subject of the camera zooming in for the money shot.

"Oh, it's real, all right." He shook his head. Looking around to see who was in hearing distance, he lowered his voice. "She offered me more money not to quit."

"More money than two-thousand dollars a day? Damn!" Slade let out a whistle.

"Maybe I'm in the wrong business." Jenna laughed.

Slade raised a brow. "Don't even think about it."

"What if we made them together? Bet you'd be all over

that."

Mustang held up one hand to silence them. "Okay, enough of this talk, please. I live in this town."

Jenna shook her head. "Boy oh boy. For a man who didn't even own a cell phone until about a month ago, you sure do get interesting phone calls."

As if on cue, his phone rang again. He glanced down and shoved it back into his pocket. Sage. That one he couldn't answer in front of Jenna.

"Who was that? It was Sage, wasn't it?" Jenna sat forward in her seat.

"Nope." Mustang shook his head and shoved the phone deeper into his jeans.

"Yes, it was. Why didn't you answer it?"

"Because knowing you, you'd grab it out of my hand and introduce yourself, and then invite her to breakfast."

"And? What would be wrong with that? Give me that phone." Jenna jumped up and started a search of his pocket in an attempt to grab his cell.

Mustang couldn't even begin to fathom what a bad idea Jenna calling Sage was. He'd never had to introduce a former lover to his current girlfriend before. There may be some etiquette for that situation, but he sure as hell didn't know it.

Of course, he couldn't explain any of that to Jenna as she managed to tickle him in an attempt to get his phone. Laughing and getting annoyed at the same time, he ended up with her in his lap still looking for his phone.

"Ow, ow, ow. My arm."

"Oh my God. I'm so sorry. Are you okay?" She jumped up and Mustang grinned.

"I'm fine. Just faking. Now sit down and act like a

grownup."

"Um, Mustang. Maybe you should have answered that call." Slade stared past him, looking at the front door of the diner.

Mustang frowned. "Why?"

"What's Sage look like?" Slade asked.

What was this about now?

"Cute. Dark hair. Brown eyes. About half a head shorter than me. About a C-cup, I'd guess." He held up his hand as if palming two breasts.

Jenna rolled her eyes at that last description.

"She drive one of those tiny little cars that the tree-huggers like? A white one." Slade asked.

This wasn't sounding good. "Yeah, why?"

Slade shook his head. "I think she was here. She saw you with Jenna in your lap, ran out the door and just peeled down Main Street."

"Shit." Mustang jumped up from his seat, wrestling his phone out of his pocket as he ran for the door. He hit redial but her voicemail came on so he left a message.

"Sage. Listen, I know it looks bad, but Jenna's just a friend. Call me back. We have to talk."

He walked back to the table, head hanging.

"I'm so sorry. If I'd known..." Jenna appeared miserable.

"I know. Not your fault." He sighed. "Maybe it's for the best."

Slade frowned. "How?"

"She's in college and working here in town. What future do we have together?" Mustang looked at Jenna. "You can work from the road, but I can't drag Sage away from her life here to follow me around the country."

"That decision is for her to make, isn't it?" Jenna pointed out.

Mustang let out a bitter laugh. "She's barely twenty, Jenna. Did you make intelligent decisions when you were that age?"

Jenna considered that for a moment. "Looking back, no. But at the time I thought so. You two need to talk, not just about today, but about your future."

"We'll talk." The question was would Sage listen?

Chapter Seventeen

Sage picked up the phone as it rang but didn't answer. She watched Mustang's name come up on the screen and then, after what seemed like an eternity of ringing, heard the chime for a new voicemail sound.

He'd left her a message? He, who had another woman in his lap while they both laughed, had bothered to leave a message?

A glutton for punishment, she slowed the car to a safe speed and hit the button to listen.

"Jenna's just a friend," Mustang's voicemail had said.

Jenna. The same name that had come up on his phone last night. At least now she knew what this Jenna looked like, not that it made her feel any better.

Sage hit the button for erase so she wouldn't be tempted to torture herself and listen to it again.

Driving aimlessly, she fought back tears. If she went home now her grandmother would know immediately that something was wrong.

She parked the car near the lake. This spot was as painful as any other as far as memories of her and Mustang were concerned. Everywhere she looked were reminders of him. She'd probably never be able to eat in the diner ever again.

This was good, really. Exactly what she needed. A dose of reality to prove to her fairytales don't exist. She knew going into this with a ladies' man like Mustang was risky.

Sage had been burying her head in the sand for weeks now, avoiding phone calls from Rosemary so she could stay in denial and forget he'd already been with her sister before he'd been with her. She hadn't wanted reality to intrude and ruin her fantasy with Mustang.

Pressing one hand against the sick, empty feeling in her stomach, Sage tried to swallow back the tears, but it was useless. She cried it all out and then got out of the car and splashed the cool lake water on her face.

After checking her reflection in the rearview mirror, Sage headed for home. She'd only have to get past her grandmother and make it to her room, then she'd be fine. Homework was always a good excuse for locking herself away for the day. Grams would leave her alone then.

What she hadn't planned on was what seeing Mustang's trailer parked next to her house would do to her. She wanted to run in and let him convince her it was all a mistake. She wanted to believe him, sink back into his arms and into the fairytale.

With a deep breath, Sage opened the front door and came face-to-face with a pacing Mustang. He stopped mid-step and spun to face the door. "Sage. I've been waiting."

She looked around. "Where's Grams?"

She didn't know how long she could hold herself together with him there. What did it mean that he'd dumped Jenna in town and come running to explain things to her? Sage tried not to read into that. She didn't dare hope.

"She got a call from the church that they needed help sorting some donations for the tag sale or something." He let out a deep breath. "Anyway, she left. We're alone and I'm glad, because we need to talk."

Mustang never got to start his talk because a knock sounded on the frame of the door she'd left open behind her.

"Hey, Sage. You're a tough girl to get in touch with."

With a last look at Mustang, Sage turned toward the door. What else could come at her all at once? "Hi, Jeremy. Sorry, I've been busy."

"That's okay. I think you should get your cell phone checked out though, because I called a bunch of times and even left messages. When you didn't get back to me I figured it must be broken."

"Yeah. Must be. I'll get it checked."

He finally acknowledged Mustang himself since Sage had made no attempt to introduce them. He stepped forward. "Hey, I'm Jeremy."

Mustang shook his extended hand. "Mustang."

"He's a neighbor. He grew up on the next street," Sage explained, knowing calling him just a neighbor belittled what they had together and at the moment not caring.

"Pleasure to meet you. Anyway, I came by because I was cleaning out my car the other day and I found this." Jeremy whipped a lipstick out of his pocket and held it up with a smile. "I know it's not mine, so I figured it must be yours. I guess you dropped it the other night on our date."

Sage watched the mixed emotions cross Mustang's face. "Thanks. I appreciate you dropping it off."

"No problem at all." With a quick glance at Mustang, as if he was deciding if he wanted an audience for what he was about to say, Jeremy continued. "So I'll call you, you know, when you get your phone fixed. There are some good movies coming out I thought we could see."

What was she supposed to say? She hadn't even really given this guy a fair chance and Mustang was leaving, not to mention messing around with another woman. "Okay."

Jeremy's face lit up. "Great. I'll see you soon then."

She nodded and repeated with far less enthusiasm. "Great."

How could she go back to a normal life, to a normal guy like Jeremy, after being with Mustang? All else paled compared to life with him.

"All right. Okay, then. Bye for now. Oh, and nice meeting you, Mustang."

"Yeah. You too." His voice sounded flat.

The door closed behind Jeremy and Sage was alone with Mustang once again. Her heart began to pound. Half of her prayed he'd step forward and take her into his arms and make it all okay.

Instead, he stayed at a safe distance all the way across the room.

"You wanted to talk?" she finally asked when he made no move to start the conversation.

"Yeah. I'm leaving town. I wanted to say goodbye."

Mustang drove the short distance to his parents' house fighting the urge to pull over and vomit. How could doing the right thing make a man feel so bad?

Sage had had someone in her life before he'd shown up. If he hadn't come back to town, if he hadn't let himself play around with both her body and her heart, she'd still be with that Jeremy guy and happy instead of hurt and miserable.

He could still see the pain on her face when he told her he was leaving. It sucked for both of them, but once he was out of the picture she'd go back to her nerdy bookworm boyfriend. They were perfect for each other actually. A man with a high-school education who made his living hanging onto a ton of bucking bull had no future with a college-educated pre-school teacher. She needed a man who liked to read books and see artsy movies and stuff.

Jeremy was as good for Sage as Mustang was bad, but saying goodbye to her was the hardest thing he'd ever done. In fact, it made the next dreaded task on his list look like a cakewalk.

Mustang parked behind the house and walked in through the kitchen door. "Ma, where's Dad? I have to talk to him."

"He's right in the living room, darlin'. Is somethin' wrong?"

Besides the hole where his heart used to be? "No. It's just I decided to go back on the road and travel with the circuit. I'm getting closer to being healed. The sports medicine docs will keep an eye on my arm. This way I'm there and ready when they say I can ride again."

His father appeared in the doorway. "So you make a decision and just up and leave? Just like that with no notice and no consideration for anyone else but yourself. What am I supposed to tell them at work?"

Mustang drew in a deep, steadying breath. "Tell them thank you very much for the job and the opportunity. I really appreciate it, but it's time I got back to my life."

His father snorted and left the room.

"Is there an address I can mail your last paycheck to?" Mustang's mother kept her voice low. So did he when he answered her. No need to tempt further wrath from the unhappy man in the other room. Better to let him stew in silence.

"Can I just leave you a deposit slip? My account's at the bank in town."

"Of course, darlin'. No problem."

He wrapped his arms around his mother. "I'm gonna miss you, Ma."

"Me too. And why aren't you wearing your sling?"

She was changing the subject. That was best for both of them. He knew she was fighting tears and he was pretty close himself. "I'll go put it on."

"You see that you do. Brisket for dinner. Will you be here to eat?"

"Yeah, I'll make sure I am. I'll leave in the morning."

She nodded and went back to the counter to finish whatever she was doing and Mustang was free to...what? Wallow?

He went to his room and took out his cell phone. He hit a button and listened.

"Hello?"

"Hey, Slade."

"Hey, what happened? Did you work things out with Sage?"

"Um, we can talk about that when I get there."

"Get where?"

"The next venue is this coming weekend in Weatherford, right?"

"Sure is."

"I'm heading out in the morning. I'll be waiting for you whenever you get there."

Slade was silent for a second. "Okay. We were going to hang out at my father's for a bit longer, but since you'll be there we'll take off early too. I'll call you when we get to Weatherford."

"Talk to you then."

Yup, this was good. Back to normal. Life on the road. Traveling with the circuit. Being around Slade and the guys again. He couldn't wait.

Mustang rubbed his stomach and wondered if his mother had any antacids in the house.

Chapter Eighteen

He entered the bar nearest the arena and saw he was not the first to arrive in town. The crews always got to the venues early to set up the chutes and pens, get the stock settled, basically get everything ready for the event.

Good. Lots of action would keep him occupied. Maybe with enough distraction he'd stop feeling shitty. Of course, enough beer would help that too. Mustang planted his ass on an empty barstool and ordered one.

"Mustang Jackson. You back already?" One of the network announcers slapped him on the back.

"Hey, JW. I'm not riding but yeah, I'm back."

JW smiled. "Missed the life, huh?"

"Something like that."

Mustang's beer arrived and JW pushed a twenty across the bar. "Get me one of those and take them both out of here."

Not one to look a gift horse in the mouth, particularly now that he was once again unemployed, Mustang raised his bottle in salute. "Thanks, man. Appreciate it."

"My pleasure. It goes on my expense account, anyway."

"Even better." Mustang grinned.

The man settled himself on the stool next to Mustang and turned sideways to face him. "I'm glad I ran into you. We've been kicking around the idea of having an announcer down by the chutes for the duration of the event. You know, catching the guys when they first get off the bull, getting comments from the riders on the leader board, which as you know changes with pretty much every ride."

Mustang nodded. "Yeah, sounds like a good plan. The fans will eat that up."

"I think so too. I also think you might be our man."

Swallowing the mouthful of beer before he spit it out at that suggestion, Mustang frowned. "Me? I don't have experience."

"The camera loves you."

That wasn't the first time Mustang had heard that in the past few days, but he was fairly certain Missy Love hadn't been talking about his face when she'd said it.

JW continued. "How about we try it out Friday night. If it doesn't work, we'll forget about the whole thing. If it does, you can be our man on the ground for the rest of the time you're out of competition. How long is that anyway?"

"Coupla more months, give or take."

"So what ya say? We'll pay you, of course. I'll have to talk to the network about how much."

Getting paid to hang around the chutes and not ride? Wow. For the first time in a long time, Mustang could visualize a life after he'd retired from bull riding. A career he wouldn't loathe, one he would actually love and be able to make a living doing. *If* things worked out Friday night.

Grinning, he extended his right hand. "All right. It's a deal."

JW sealed the agreement with a handshake. "Wonderful."

Nearly a week without Mustang. It felt more like a month. Considering that, how come she didn't feel any better?

Probably because even now, rather than calling Jeremy and seeing if he wanted to go out, Sage sat on the edge of her bed waiting for the bull ride to come on. What she was watching for, she didn't know.

Did she really want to catch him on camera with his *friend* Jenna in his lap again? Actually, she did. Maybe that would knock some sense into her. She was pitiful. Absolutely pitiful. That still didn't prevent her from leaning forward when the announcer's voice came on.

"We have a special treat for the folks at home tonight, Jim. Mustang Jackson, who you might remember was taken out of competition last month when Ballbreaker snapped his ulna and sent him to the hospital for surgery, is going to be our man on the ground today."

What? Mustang was now an announcer? When had that happened?

"That's right, JW. Mustang's back with the tour, but Doc Tandy from the sports medicine team confirms he won't be back on a bull for a good two months."

"Exactly, but Mustang is willing to take a stab at being on the other side of the microphone tonight. He'll be interviewing the riders down on the arena floor, behind the chutes and most likely in back with the Doc. And we know the sports medicine room is a place Mustang is mighty familiar with."

"I can hear you guys up there you know, and I'd like it noted that I've spent less time in the infirmary than most." Mustang's voice startled Sage.

She stood and got as close to the set as she could without distorting the picture. Then there he was, those intense eyes she'd stared into every time they'd made love, those lips that

197

had covered most of her body.

The two other announcers laughed. "Hey, Mustang. This is Jim. What do you anticipate being the biggest challenge for you in your new role tonight?"

"That's easy, Jim. It will be getting some of these cowboys to talk. Bull riders aren't big talkers generally. Stick a microphone in the face of one after he's just eaten a face full of dirt before the buzzer and I'm likely to end up back with Doc Tandy."

Jim laughed. "That'll keep you quick on your feet, at least."

"Sure will," Mustang agreed, holding the earpiece but remembering to look at the camera, which meant he appeared to be looking right at Sage.

JW took over the questioning. "The first of the riders is in the chutes. It's last year's Rookie of the Year, Chase Reese, aboard Jersey Boy. Mustang. Who do you pick in this match up?"

"That's a tough one, JW. If Chase keeps his eyes where they belong, he should be good to go and have no problem with a bull like Jersey Boy."

"He's given the nod and off they go... Aw, and he's in the dirt. What happened there, Mustang?"

The camera cut to Mustang, who was shaking his head. "He looked at the ground. If you look there you're gonna go there."

"Can you get us a few words with Chase, Mustang?"

"I'll sure give it a try." Mustang pulled the mic away from his face and yelled, "Hey, Chase."

The look on the young cowboy's face was nearly comical when Mustang came at him with the microphone.

"Uh hey, Mustang." His eyes cut to the camera with a bit of

a deer-in-headlights look.

"Hey, kid. Good to see you again. Do you know what went wrong out there?"

The rider focused back on Mustang and took in a deep breath full of frustration. "Yeah, I know. I looked down, just like you told me not to."

Mustang slapped him on the back. "You have a plan for next time?"

"Yeah, I'm not gonna look down."

"Good." He grinned encouragement at the kid and then looked at the camera. "Back to you guys in the booth."

JW laughed. "We didn't know we had the Zen master of bull riding down there on the floor."

Jim agreed. "You're not kidding, JW. Let's take a look at Garret James next, aboard Full House. Any thoughts on this one, Mustang?"

"Well, Jim, they've got a right-handed rider loaded for a left-side delivery. Chances are that bull is gonna go left out of the chute, away from Garret's hand. That can be a problem for the younger kids like Garret with less experience."

"Great observation, Mustang. Let's see how he does."

The banter continued as Sage stayed glued to the screen. She wanted to hate him, at least to forget him. But watching how he mentored the younger riders, really seeming to care, softened the heart she hadn't done a very good job of hardening against him. Hearing his laugh, seeing his smile, only made her miss him more.

There was a lull in the action and Mustang went into the stands and sat down next to none other than Jenna. Sage's heart lodged firmly in her throat as Mustang spoke, "I'd like to introduce someone to you guys. JW, Jim, America, this is

Jenna Block, Slade Bower's girlfriend. Say hello to the viewers and the boys in the booth, darlin'."

Jenna was Mustang's best friend's girlfriend. He hadn't been lying. She was just a friend. Sage watched open-mouthed as the woman appeared shocked at being put on the spot on camera.

"Slade Bower is the rider currently ranked second in the world and has yet to ride tonight. Mustang, can you ask Miss Block how she's feeling about watching her boyfriend get on the bull that put Skeeter in the hospital not long ago?"

Mustang opened his mouth to relay the question when Slade stalked into the shot. "Mustang, what the fu—"

"And here's the man himself. Slade, turn to the camera and say hello to the folks watching at home."

The men in the announcer's booth laughed. "Good job keeping us G-rated for the sensors on Mustang's part."

Laughing, Mustang managed to get fairly coherent comments from both Slade and his girlfriend as Sage sat shakily on the bed.

Sage's mind began to reel. If he hadn't left because he wanted to be with Jenna instead of her, then why had he? He must have gone because she overreacted. She hadn't even let him explain.

She had to apologize. Tonight.

Where the hell were they again? Weatherford? She could get there in a few hours. Decision made, Sage began throwing clothes into a bag.

About to climb the stairs and unlock the door of his trailer,

Mustang felt a tap on his shoulder. He turned and found the last person he'd expected to see. The only person he really wanted to be there. "Sage."

"I'm so sorry. I should have trusted you. I should have believed you when you called and left the message saying Jenna was just a friend." She started crying before she even finished the apology.

He pulled her into his arms. It felt really good to hold her. "Shh. It's okay."

"It's not okay. You left. Months before you had to, you left because of me. Because I wouldn't let you explain about who she was."

"Sage, I could have gotten you to listen. Hell, I would have made you hear me out, but when I met Jeremy I realized you had a nice, steady guy who should be your boyfriend instead of me. You need someone like him." Mustang swept his arm to encompass his surroundings. The arena, the trailer, the bar. "This is my life. I can't ask you to make it yours."

"You left so I could be with Jeremy? We're only friends."

He laughed. "He doesn't want to be just friends, believe me."

"It doesn't matter what he wants because I want you."

"I want you too, but I can't be selfish. You have to finish school. You need a guy with a real job and a steady paycheck and a pension plan and, hell, I don't know, a 401K."

"I don't want any of that. I just want you."

Mustang shook his head. "There's a lot you don't know about me, Sage. I've done some things I'm not proud of."

She held on to him more tightly. "I've done things I'm not proud of too."

He let out a short laugh. "I seriously doubt that."

"Look, I don't care what you did before we were together."

"You can't say that because you don't know." Mustang shook his head, totally torn.

Jenna had been right. He and Sage couldn't start a serious relationship by keeping things from each other. On the other hand, Mustang had done most things long before he'd reconnected with Sage.

That stuff didn't affect him and Sage. The brief thing he'd had with Jenna and Slade would never be repeated and had happened months before Sage had reentered his life. Besides, it wasn't only his story to tell. Jenna had a reputation to maintain.

But the things that had happened after he'd started building a relationship with Sage, that he would confess.

"Listen to me. I don't care." She enunciated each word carefully. "All I care about is you."

"I care about you too. More than anything else. That's why I want to tell you what I've done. I want to start our lives together with a clean slate."

Or as clean as his very dirty slate could get.

"Can't we just go inside and be together. Start our lives over. I don't want to talk about the past." She looked frightened. He didn't blame her. He was frightened too.

"Let's go inside, but we are going to talk."

"Okay."

Mustang opened the door and let her go in before him. She sat on the bed. That nearly distracted him enough to say fuck it to his confession and sink into her. He couldn't do that. He owed her this.

"You know those two Saturdays I couldn't see you?"

"Yes."

He swallowed. This was harder than he thought it would be. She could easily walk away from him and never look back after this, but he had to do it. "Well, when I'd told you it was work, that was the truth. I took a job I'm not very proud of..."

And that began the whole sordid tale. He spared her the worst of the details and kept just to the facts. The bare basics of what he'd done and why were enough. He'd had sex on camera for money. She didn't need to know any more than that. His having those images in his brain was enough. Sage didn't need them too.

After he was done she sat in silence for a good minute. To Mustang it felt more like an eternity.

"So you had sex with other women."

"Yes."

"After you had sex with me?"

"No. Before. They called and asked me to do another one after I'd been with you and I said no. I couldn't, I wouldn't do that."

"Why?"

"Because I couldn't be with another woman, even for money, after I'd been with you. I didn't want to. The only woman I want now is you." His pulse racing, he added, "If you'll have me."

She drew in a shaky breath and shook her head. "I think I need some time."

"I understand." He rose. "I'll see about getting you a hotel room. You probably won't want to stay here with me."

He waited, but the response he got was a nod as she rose and headed for the door. He let her go. What else could he do?

Feeling ill, Sage headed blindly across the street and into the bar. Ignoring everything as she concentrated solely on getting into the bathroom before she broke down, she kept her head down and didn't look at any of the other patrons she passed along the way.

She made it in the door before the first tear escaped. She eyed the stiff brown paper in the wall dispenser.

"Here." A woman she hadn't noticed inside handed her a tissue.

Glancing up, she recognized Jenna immediately. "Um, Thanks."

"Man trouble?"

Sage laughed through her tears. "Yeah. How'd you know?"

"I've shed a few tears in public restrooms myself over a certain cowboy, but the good news is now he's waiting for me outside and things are wonderful."

She was talking about Slade. Sage wasn't sure she could see wonderful in her future with Mustang, not as long as she couldn't see past what he'd just told her.

"Come on. I'll buy you a drink."

"I'm not old enough to drink."

Jenna laughed. "Oh, to be young again. Then I'll buy you a soda. You look like you could use someone to talk to."

Sage shook her head. "I should probably just go find a hotel room."

"That might not be so easy with the competition in town. Did you travel far to get here?"

"I just drove in from Texas."

"Really? Where abouts? Slade is from Texas."

"Magnolia."

Jenna's eyes opened wide. "Um, this may sound like a crazy question, but your name doesn't happen to be Sage, does it?"

"Yeah." How did Jenna know her name?

"I'm a friend of Mustang's. He's told me all about you. I'm Jenna Block."

"He told you about me?"

"Of course he did. Well, I mean he didn't want to because God forbid Mustang admit he's fallen hard for a girl, but yeah, he finally admitted it."

"He's fallen hard for me?"

Jenna nodded. "Oh, yeah. Do *not* tell him I said this but he's got it bad for you. It's like he's a totally different man since he's met you."

Sage realized her tears had stopped. She held up the tissue. "Thanks for this, and for the talk."

"You're very welcome. So, how about that soda? I'm sure Slade would love to meet you too."

"Thanks, but I think I have a cowboy of my own I need to go see." She'd waited too long for him to be in her life. She wasn't going to waste one more moment of it.

"I totally understand. Maybe we'll see you tomorrow morning. We can all do breakfast, the four of us."

Sage smiled. "I'd like that."

Chapter Nineteen

"No availability at all?" Mustang sighed in frustration. "Okay, thanks."

He'd just disconnected when there was a light tap on the door. Jumping for the door, he flung it open. "Sage."

"Hi."

"Hi." His heart fluttered. "Do you want to come in?"

She nodded. "Did you get a hotel room for tonight yet?" Sage fidgeted with the strap of her bag.

Mustang held up the phone. "Not yet. The two closest to the arena are booked, but I'm about to start calling the ones a little farther into town."

"You don't have to. I don't want a hotel room. I want to stay here with you." She raised her eyes to meet his.

"Are you sure?"

"Yeah. Very sure." Dropping her bag on the floor, she took a step forward. "I need you to know it makes me insane even thinking about you with another woman, but I understand why you did it. I know what worrying about your future and working with your father did to you. And I know that having you in my life, no matter how difficult, has to be better than not having you at all. I tried living without you. I didn't like it."

He ran both hands up and down her arms and lowered his

forehead to rest against hers. "How'd you get so wise so young, Little Bit?"

She pulled back, a wrinkle marring her brow. "That's another thing. It bothers me how you still insist on calling me *Little Bit* when I've heard you call my sister and Jenna and who knows who else darlin'."

He laughed. "Ah, Sage. I call nearly every woman I meet *darlin'*, but you are the only one in the world I've ever called Little Bit. Does that make you feel any better about it?"

Her expression softened and he swore her eyes looked glassy. "Yeah, it does."

"Good. But there's still something bothering me. This is a tough life, Sage. I'm on the road all the time. Jenna travels with Slade a lot, but you can't do that. You have school—"

"I take classes online, Mustang. I can do that from anywhere."

"But your job—"

"Is almost over for this year, then I have a nice long summer break. Besides, I've been kind of thinking about switching my major. I'm really enjoying my psych classes. If I do change, I won't be student teaching anymore."

"You have an answer for everything, don't you?" Mustang grinned.

"Not really. I'm not sure what I want to do with school or work. Maybe I'll take a year off to think about it. All I know is I want to be with you. You have a problem with that?" Sage smirked.

"Not a bit. My only problem is that big bed behind me that I've spent too many nights in without you. I don't intend on spending another one. That okay with you?"

Sage nodded. "Yeah, I'm very okay."

About the Author

As an award-winning author of contemporary erotic romance in genres including military, cowboy, ménage and paranormal, Cat Johnson uses her computer so much she wore the letters off the keyboard within a year. She is known for her creative marketing and research practices. Consequently, Cat owns an entire collection of camouflage shoes for book signings and a fair number of her consultants wear combat and cowboy boots for a living. In her real life, she's been a marketing manager, professional harpist, bartender, tour guide, radio show host, Junior League president, sponsor of a bull-riding rodeo cowboy, wife and avid animal lover.

To learn more about Cat Johnson, please visit www.catjohnson.net. Send an email to cat at catjohnson.net or join her MySpace at www.myspace.com/authorcatjohnson or her Facebook at www.facebook.com/authorcatjohnson. Follow Cat on Twitter at www.twitter.com/cat_johnson.

When country boys meet a city girl, everyone is in for a wild ride.

Unridden
© *2009 Cat Johnson*
Studs in Spurs, Book 1

Slade Bower and Mustang Jackson are living the high life on the professional bull-riding circuit. The prize money is big, the bulls are rank and the women are willing. But something is missing.

For Slade, waking up in a different city with a different woman each morning is holding less and less appeal. Even Mustang's creative attempts to shake things up don't help. Then along comes a big-city author who's like nothing they've ever encountered. Something about her makes Slade sit up and take notice—and Mustang is always up for anything.

Romance writer Jenna Block has a problem—her agent thinks a cowboy book will jump-start her career. A born New Yorker, Jenna doesn't do cowboys, not on paper, and definitely not in real life. Luckily for her there are two cowboys ready, willing and able to take her out of her comfort zone in every way that counts...and some ways she hadn't counted on.

Warning: This story contains two hot cowboys, one very lucky woman, hot ménage sex and lots of bull.

Available now in ebook and print from Samhain Publishing.

Enjoy the following excerpt from Unridden...

Evaluating that night's possibilities, Mustang's gaze swept the females in the stands until it landed on one woman who made him stop dead in his perusal.

He jumped up onto the rail of the chute and hissed to Slade, "Second section, fourth row back, reddish-brown hair pulled back in a ponytail, black turtleneck."

In the process of tugging the rope that stretched beneath the bull and winding it once around his gloved hand, Slade frowned up at Mustang from the animal's back. "I'm in the middle of taking my wrap and you're pointing out some woman to me? In a turtleneck, no less? Since when are you interested in women whose chest isn't hanging out?"

"This woman's different, Slade. I can tell." The bull hopped once in the chute and Mustang quickly reached over and grabbed the back of Slade's vest, steadying him on the animal's back.

"Dammit, Mustang, quit distracting me." Slade settled himself again and then gave a nod. The cowboy on the ground swung the gate open to release both bull and rider into the arena.

"Talk to you more when you get off," Mustang called after him.

As Mustang watched his friend disappear into a cloud of dust, Chase Reese hopped up onto the rail next to him.

"Slade's amazing. It's like he's glued onto that bull. I wish I could do that. I went two for ten last series." The kid had been favored for Rookie of the Year until he'd hit a dry streak.

"That's because you look at the ground." Mustang followed

Slade's progress while the bull spun around to the left without deviation, from one end of the arena to the other.

The eight-second buzzer sounded and Slade released the rope wrapped around his hand. He jumped off the bull, hit the ground with his shoulder and then rolled to avoid a hoof to the ribcage before the bullfighters redirected the charging animal away from him.

"I do what?"

Seeing his friend was safe, Mustang took the time to answer Chase's question. Damn, had he ever been this young? The kid probably didn't even have to shave once a week.

"You're looking down at the ground while you ride. If you look there, you're gonna end up there. It's a fact. Now, 'scuse me. I gotta talk to Slade."

Leaving the kid with an amazed expression on his face, as if he'd just been handed all the secrets of the universe, Mustang jumped down to go meet Slade behind the chutes.

"Hey, man. Good ride. That bull was one hell of a spinner, huh?"

Slade laughed and pulled the tape from around his wrist where it held the glove on his riding hand firmly in place. "Hell yeah. They weren't kidding when they said he came out of the spinner pen. Felt like I was on a ride at the county fair."

"Now we're both done riding for the night, we have to formulate a plan," Mustang began.

"For what?"

"To reel in that woman I told you about."

Slade dismissed that with a wave of his hand. "Just do whatever it is you usually do."

Mustang shook his head. "The usual isn't going to work on her."

Slade sighed. "Where did you say she's sitting?"

Ha! Slade had given in and was actually showing some interest. Smiling, Mustang narrowed his eyes and easily found her again in the stands. She was writing feverishly while trying to watch the rider in the arena at the same time. He tilted his head toward the section directly behind them. "Far end of the fourth row."

"What the hell is she doing?" Slade frowned as he watched her.

"Hell if I know, but I think she's taking notes. See what I mean? This woman is special. She isn't going to just fall into our bed."

Her hair wasn't huge, she wasn't made up like a showgirl and her clothes showed curves but not an inch of skin. She was different, which was what had drawn Mustang's attention to her in the first place.

Since Slade had been in his strange funk lately, Mustang figured he'd try something unusual. Hell, even the two eighteen-year-olds going at each other in front of them barely got a rise out of his friend. Mustang was running out of ideas, but this woman... She was pretty much the opposite of their usual conquest and that might be exactly what they needed. It was worth a shot to cheer Slade up. Besides, never opposed to trying new things, he could use a bit of a change himself once in a while.

"Mustang, she's probably a damned reporter. That's all I need, to be featured in some exposé. I can see the headline now. 'Slade Bower, third-ranking bull rider in the world, propositions reporter for a threesome with former Rookie of the Year, Mustang Jackson.' That will go over real well with the fans in the Bible Belt." Slade scowled at Mustang. "Pick someone else. How about the one bouncing up and down over there? She's about to pop right out of that top. You might want to keep an eye on her."

Mustang glanced her way. "Yeah, I saw her already. I'm set on the other one."

Laughing, Slade shook his head. "Good luck 'cause I can just about see the stick up her ass from here. That one is wound tight, but you go for it, man, and I'll enjoy watching you get shot down."

Mustang raised a brow. "Is that a challenge, my friend?"

Slade let out a short laugh. "No, it's the truth."

"Well, I think you're wrong. Sometimes it's the quiet ones that are the wildest once you get them naked."

"And you think you can get her naked?"

Mustang nodded. "Yup. I do."

"Well, I'd like to see that."

Grinning, Mustang slapped his friend on the back. "Don't worry. You'll be there too."

Slade shook his head. "*Maybe*, and that is a big maybe, you might be able to get that woman naked, with enough alcohol and bull, but no frigging way will she agree to both of us. Never in a million years."

Feeling cocky and never one to resist a challenge, Mustang crossed his arms and dug in his heels. "We'll see. You willing to make a bet on that?"

He held the reins to her heart once—and this time he won't let go.

The Real Deal
© *2009 Niki Green*
A Wild Ride story.

Willa Tate left Millbrook, Texas, years ago—along with her future, her fiancé and her heart. Now, as one of the headlining acts at a hot burlesque club, she looks into the crowd, sees a familiar face staring up at her—and her past comes crashing back.

Chase Kiel has some hard questions for the former love of his life. He spent forever looking for her, and now he wants answers—even if he has to throw her over his shoulder and drag her back to Millbrook to get them.

He'd find it a hell of a lot easier if the chemistry weren't still there. If they didn't still fit together like keg of dynamite and fuse. If he didn't want not only his answers...but her heart.

Chase is still certain he and Willa belong together—and convincing Willa of it will be his pleasure.

Warning: This title contains explicit, powder-keg-hot sex, language that ain't fit for your mama's ears, and a hot cowboy with a Texas-sized heart.

Available now in ebook from Samhain Publishing.
Also available in the print anthology Wild Ride from Samhain Publishing

HOT STUFF

Discover Samhain!

THE HOTTEST NEW PUBLISHER ON THE PLANET

Romance, fantasy, mystery, thriller, mainstream and more—Samhain has more selection, hotter authors, and everything's available in ebook.

Pick your favorite, sit back, and enjoy the ride! Hot stuff indeed.

SAMHAIN

PUBLISHING

WWW.SAMHAINPUBLISHING.COM

9 781605 049236